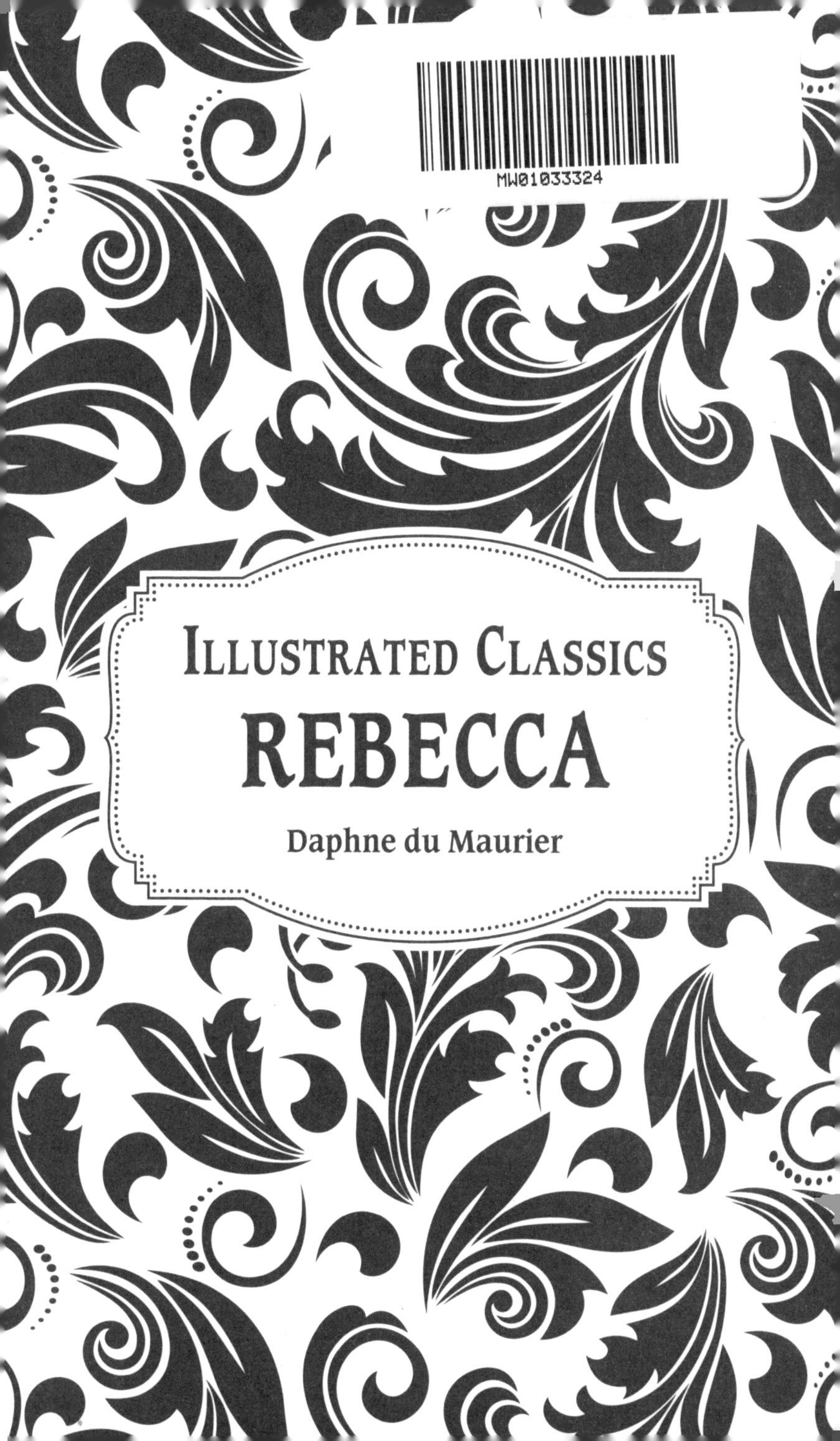
ILLUSTRATED CLASSICS
REBECCA
Daphne du Maurier

ILLUSTRATED CLASSICS

REBECCA

Daphne du Maurier

Wonder House

Originally published in 1938
This abridged edition published in 2021

(An imprint of Prakash Books)

contact@wonderhousebooks.com

ISBN : 9789354403460

Contents

About the Book

Best described as a gothic novel, *Rebecca* is a suspense and psychological thriller about a young, woman wealthy American woman who is on a holiday.

While on her vacation in Monte Carlo, she meets a handsome widower, Maximillian de Winter. His proposal takes her by surprise and she soon finds herself in his Cornish estate, the well-know Manderley, as Mrs de Winter.

At the estate, she finds herself haunted by the memory of the deceased first Mrs de Winter, Rebecca. Though dead, Rebecca's mannerisms are deeply imbibed by the servants. They are not willing to change and continue to follow the diktats laid down by Rebecca. The sinister housekeeper at Manderley, Mrs Danvers, adds to her agony reminding the young mistress of her inferiority. She resents the new Mrs de Winter, which is openly evident, making her feel lowly and menial.

As the novel unfolds, the true Rebecca begins to reveal herself and events unfurl into a nail-biting finish.

Described as one of the most influential novels of the twentieth century, this tale ensures that it keeps the reader on the edge till the very last word is read.

About the Author

Daphne Du Maurier was born in London in 1907 to an actress mother and an actor-manager father. Along with her two sisters, she was home schooled by governesses and grew up in a world of fantasy, story, and imagination.

The family's holidays at their country home made Daphne du Maurier develop an everlasting love for Cornwall, which became the backdrop of many of her stories.

In 1931, she published her first novel *The Loving Spirit.* In 1935, she was recognized as a writer to reckon with when she wrote an honest biography about her father titled *Gerald: A Portrait. Jamaica Inn* in 1936 made it to the bestseller charts. She married Major Frederick Browning in 1932. She wrote *Rebecca* in 1938 which became her best known work. Alfred Hitchcock made *Rebecca* into a movie in 1940. Two of her other novels, *Frenchman's Creek* and *Hungry Hill,* also became popular films.

She was honored by the title Dame of the British Empire in 1969. She believed that writers should be read, neither seen nor heard, and once you pick her work you will read until the end—until all sense is gently awakened.

She died in 1989 in Cornwall.

Chapter 1

Manderley

Last night I dreamt I went to Manderley again. The iron gates were barred to me. Suddenly, as if controlled by mystical powers, I entered like a spirit. The drive was not as we knew it. Nature had wound its way and encroached upon it with long obstinate fingers. The woods that bordered the drive seemed dark and wild. The huge branches of the beeches intertwined with one another making a gigantic archway like the vault of a Church above my head.

As the drive narrowed, the branches of the tress grew lower making progress an obstacle and the twisted roots looked like skeleton claws, the lovely blue hydrangeas grew tall and ugly with no blooms whatsoever. Beyond them all stood the glorious Manderley. As I stood there with a thumping heart and a sting of tears behind my eyes, I saw the gray stone building, silent and secretive, which shone in the moonlight like a silent jewel.

The terrace sloped to the lawns and the lawns stretched to the sea, placid waters under the silver moon. The garden lay in disarray with rhododendron having grown wild. The ivy seemed to be creeping across the lawns engulfing the house. Nettles, like forerunners in an army were everywhere, but enthralled as I was in my dream I marched on. The house seemed, not like an empty shell, but alive and breathing.

Light streamed through the vertical windows and the curtains swayed gently in the breeze. The library would be just as we had left it, books, newspapers, cushions strewn, ashtrays, and our dear Jasper, thumping his tail at the sound of his master's footsteps.

Then, a cloud cast its shadow upon the moon, and it was as if the house had been thrown into a desolate darkness again. The house was like a grave in which suffering and fear were buried.

In my waking hours I would not be bitter about Manderley. Instead, I would remember its beautiful rose garden, the murmur of the sea, tea under the chestnut tree and the Happy Valley.

However, these were but a dream, for, in reality, we were many miles away in an unfamiliar land in a plain bedroom of a hotel. An ordinary day stretched before us, with a serenity that we did not mind, for Manderley was a thing of the past, ours no more.

Chapter 2

The Aftermath

Never can we go back to Manderley again. The past with its fear and unrest is hopefully behind us. He does often look lost and perplexed. There are signs, there is a displaced look, a quick talking about nothing, excessive smoking, a kind of therapy to the hurt and agony of the past.

They say that in order to progress man must suffer and with the suffering emerge stronger. Mercifully, we have fought and conquered our battle. I have had enough melodrama for one life and although the past does shadow us, I do believe we are one now and forever. Happiness, a state of mind, is to be cherished and whilst moments of depression come to cloud us, we now have no secrets from each other.

Our hotel room is dull and food uninteresting, and we are bored from time to time, but its straightforwardness gives us anonymity. In a big hotel he would meet too many people he would know. We look forward to the postman bringing the English Mail because it is a grist to our starving soul. The ritual of tea continues here. Half past four at Manderley and a table would be set before the library fire. There, there was crisp toast, dripping crumpets, hot scones, delicious ginger bread, melt-in-the-mouth angel cake and all sorts of sandwiches. Here, there were two slices of bread and butter and China Tea.

The waste at Manderley sometimes worried me but I dared not have asked Mrs. Danvers for I feared I would automatically be compared to Rebecca. I wonder what Mrs. Danvers and Favell are doing these days.

In my heart there is no torment now and my faithful Jasper is happy in hunting grounds. But Manderley lies deceased, like an empty shell much as it did in my dream. Intimidating Manderley, with its deep dark woods, rustling leaves, a multitude of weeds, the cottage in the cove, the singing birds, all these make me shudder and I look with relief from our balcony at the vineyards as they sparkle in the sun. I am a woman with confidence now, much unlike the timid, shy and diffident girl that drove to Manderley for the first time, gauche and yearning to please.

What did I look like then, in comparison to Rebecca?

Chapter 3

Mrs. Van Hopper

My memory takes me back to the days when I was a mere companion to the rather large and loud Mrs. Van Hopper. While she had a short body she balanced on high heels, a new hat with a quill and walked swinging her hips, I was a shy girl with straight short hair, no make-up and an ill-fitting coat.

The little restaurant where we are today is so different from the ostentatious and ornate dining room of the Côte d'Azur in Monte Carlo. My companion now, smiles every now and then as he peels a mandarin much unlike Mrs. Van Hopper who would heap her plate with ravioli and look surreptitiously at mine to make sure that I had not had the better dish. But she had nothing to worry, for, the waiter having guessed my inferior nature had sent me a plate of dry food. I remember being treated much worst at a country house with Mrs. Van Hopper where even my tea was left stone cold outside my bedroom door.

Mrs. Van Hopper would make her way to her usual tab in the corner of the dining room and survey it lifting her lorgnette to her small pig's eyes. "Not a single well-known personality," she would say. "I must ask the management to make a reduction on my bill. Do I come here to look at th page boys?"

That afternoon, Mrs. Van Hopper was enjoying her ravioli with the sauce dripping down her chin, and I was navigating my unpalatable plate of food. It was then that the table next to ours, which had lain vacant for the past three days, was being occupied. The maître d'hôtel, with special bow reserved for special patrons seated the newcomer down. Mrs. Van Hopper indubitably stared with renewed interest at the gentleman who was concentrating over his menu, whereas I, on the other hand, blushed to see Mrs. Van Hopper's obvious curiosity.

"It's Max de Winter," she said, "the man who owns Manderley. You must have heard, haven't you? He does look ill after his wife's death, for he can't get over it…"

Had Mrs. Van Hopper not been a snob, perhaps my life would have been very different today. The snooty and nosey lady made it a point to park herself upon a sofa midway between the reception and sofa of the Co'te de' zur and use me as a bait to pounce on her prey. She would want to claim people of distinction as her friends. Apart from bridge, this was her one passion and I had to bear her indignities like a whipping boy. Often have I known of people laughing behind her back or disappearing into another room when she entered.

It was many years ago, on that unforgettable afternoon, when Mrs. Van Hopper hurried through her dessert so she could make herself ready on her sofa in the lounge for an attack on a naive victim.

Debating her means of attack, tapping her lorgnette against her teeth, she made me dash to our room to find a letter written by her nephew during his honeymoon, with snapshot. I did as was bidden, and found the letter in a pigeon hole in her desk and wished I could somehow warn him of the ambush.

I must have been away longer than I thought for Mrs. Van Hopper had caught him on his way out of the dining room and he was seated on the sofa beside her. She flapped a hand in my direction, muttered my name and instructed me to go and ask the waiter for another cup, for, "Mr. de Winter is having coffee with us," she said, her tone indicating my standing.

This gentleman, however, remained standing and said,

"You both are having coffee with me." He signaled to the waiter and before I knew what was happening, he was sitting on the hard chair usually reserved for me and I was sitting on the sofa beside her. Masking her annoyance, she was soon leaning her large self towards his chair and began her tirade, "Why, Mr. de Winter, I recognized you the minute you walked in, Billy's friend, and I must show you the snaps of Billy and his bride on their honeymoon."

This man's face was arresting, sensitive and from a medieval era. I was so lost in my thoughts of the man sitting with us that I had lost the thread of conversation and when I jolted back Mrs. Van Hopper was saying, "If Billy's home was like Manderley, which, I believe is like a fairyland, then I am certain he would not want to frolic around in Palm Beach."

Ignorant of his unsmiling face and the fine line, I noticed between his brows. Mrs. Van Hopper went on, "The pictures of the place are so charming and I can see that you cannot bear to leave it. Billy did say that it could beat any place for its beauty."

His silence seemed painful and was apparent except to Mrs. Van Hopper who continued to trample and trespass like a clumsy goat. I was flushed with the color of embarrassment flooding my cheeks.

"You Englishmen do disparage your homes so as not to seem arrogant. There's the much talked about Minstrels' gallery."

He guessed my anguish, and leaned towards me to ask if I would have more coffee. He enquired as to what I thought of Monte Carlo, much to the chagrin of Mrs. Van Hopper.

"I have not decided as I left in a hurry," he said. His face took on a clouded demeanor. Mrs. Van Hopper continued to speak of people, dropping names and titles as if they were her middle name.

All this was making the gentleman uncomfortable and disinterested but his good manners did not make him glance at his watch. When a page boy came to say that a dressmaker was waiting for Mrs. Van Hopper in her suite, Mr. Max de Winter was finally freed of his misery. We parted at the lift doors where Mrs. Van Hopper invited him the next day and he declined politely saying that he might be driving to Sospel.

As Mr. de Winter turned and left and we reached our suite Mrs. Van Hopper said, "I don't mean to be unkind but you did put yourself forward this afternoon. Your efforts to monopolies the conversation was quite disconcerting."

I said nothing. Soon bridge would begin and with it a mundane evening. I began to sketch. There was a knock at the door. A lift boy brought a note. It was not for madam but for me. Inside it was written, 'Forgive me. I was very rude this afternoon.' My name, spelt correctly, was on the envelope.

The lift boy waited to ask if there was an answer and I said there wasn't. After he left, I went back to my drawing but even that did not gratify me anymore.

Forgive Me.
I was very rude
this afternoon.

Chapter 4

Mr. Max de Winter

The next morning Mrs. Van Hopper woke up with a bout of influenza. The doctor advised that she should stay in bed and hire a trained nurse. At first, I thought the idea was ridiculous but to my surprise she agreed readily. This would create a fuss and a stir amongst her friends who would visit her and bring her flowers. Monte Carlo, which was now getting quite dull would provide some distraction.

After I had settled her in with her new nurse, propped her on pillows and rung up her friends to put off the evening party, I went down to lunch a good half hour early with a lightness in my heart which I was a little ashamed of.

I had expected the dining room to be empty considering it wasn't one yet, but the table next to ours was occupied. And, I thought he had gone to Sospel. He was lunching early; I am sure to evade us and perhaps for the same reason had avoided dinner in the restaurant yesterday.

I walked looking straight before me and paid the penalty by knocking a vase of flowers down. The water soaked the cloth and was running down my lap and before I knew what had happened, my neighbor was by my side with a dry napkin. In the clamor that followed he instructed the waiter to set another place for me at his table. I was mortified. "Please," I said, "do not be polite."

"I am not being polite," he said, "and I do want you to have lunch with me. We need not even speak to each other if you don't want to."

He enquired after Mrs. Van Hopper and I told him what had happened. He apologized for his rudeness the previous day. "You were not rude; her curiosity gets the better of her especially with people of importance," I explained.

"I am flattered, but why am I important?" he asked.

"I think your home, Manderley," I said.

The mention of his home brought a mask upon his face and I wondered why a place known to many even by hearsay should be a sore point with him. I reminisced as I ate in silence, an incident that had happened a long time ago. I had bought a picture post card when on a holiday. The painting was of a house and although it was done crudely, the beauty of the house with wide stone steps before the terrace and green lawns stretching to the sea was breathtaking. I paid two pence, half my pocket money, for it and asked the shop woman what the picture was. "That's Manderley," she said and I left the shop feeling snubbed.

I understood now, why intrusive people like Mrs. Van Hopper were disliked by him and with both our thoughts upon her he asked what my relation with her was.

"She's training me to be a companion and pays ninety pounds a year for that," I explained.

"I didn't know one could buy companionship!" he said. "Why would you do it?"

"For the ninety pounds," I replied.

"Don't you have any family?"

"No; they are dead."

"You have a lovely and unusual name."

"My father was a lovely and unusual person."

As I looked at him over my glass of citronade I wanted to tell him that my family was my secret just as Manderley was his. But like an unreal dream, twenty-four hours after yesterday, here I was with a complete stranger spilling my life before him. I told him of the vibrant personality my father was and that when he was struck with pneumonia my mother could survive not more than five weeks without him.

I realized it was almost two o'clock and I had dominated the conversation. As I began to splutter my apologies, he said that he had enjoyed the hour with me more than anything else in the past year and that it helped to lift him out of his desolation and brooding, his devils of the past year.

He said that we both had one thing in common, 'loneliness!' He had a sister whom he didn't see very much and an ancient grandmother he had to visit thrice a year.

"You forget," I said, "you have a home and I have none."

I regretted having spoken those tactless words immediately for he got that impenetrable look in his eyes again. "An empty house can be as lonely as a full hotel," he said. "The trouble is, it is less impersonal." I thought he would speak to me of Manderley but some fear seemed to be holding him back.

Suddenly, he asked what I would do with my day off and I said that I wanted to go to a cobbled square in Monaco with my sketchbook and pencil and to my dismay he said that he would drive me there.

I remembered what Mrs. Van Hopper had said about me putting myself forward and thought that he might believe the same of me. It was exactly what she would have done.

Over coffee we spoke and he asked me how old I was and when I told him he laughed. "I know this age; it makes one stubborn. Go up and put on your hat while I have the car brought out."

As I stepped into the lift, I had misjudged him and he was not at all hard or scornful. He seemed to me a friend of many years or like a brother I never possessed. That was one happy afternoon and I remember it well.

I remember the harbor with fluttering paper boats. I remember that I was wearing my most comfortable and ill-fitting flannel suite with a shabby hat and low-heeled shoes. I was clutching a pair of gauntlet gloves. I had never looked so youthful or felt so old all at the same time, my shyness having vanished. Mrs. Van Hopper, her bridge and her influenza were all forgotten.

The strong wind made sketching impossible and we bundled into the car again, climbing along a hill, dangerously fast but the danger somehow pleased me. How different was his car to that of Mrs. Van Hopper? There I would sit with my back to the driver and crane my neck to see the view. Here, the car seemed to have the wings of Mercury. I remember laughing aloud whereas he was once more disconnected and silent.

We reached the summit from where we could go no further. Below us, the road that we had navigated stretched before us, precipitous and hollow. At the edge of the road there was a sharp vertical slope of about two thousand feet. The silence between us was austere and an eerie air overcame the atmosphere. I asked nervously if he had known this place and had come here before?

He looked at me without recognition and I realized that he was lost in the web of his thoughts. He seemed to be under a spell. We were within six feet of death.

"It's getting late, we should go," I said. Coming out of his dream he saw my ashen face and apologizing said, "This was a dreadful thing for me to do." We climbed into the car while he gently maneuvered it down the slope and I clutched at my seat with both hands. "Have you been here before?" I asked.

"Yes," he said, "a long time ago and I wanted to see if it had changed."

"Has it?" I asked.

"No, it hasn't?" And I wondered what had brought on this retreat into the past.

On our drive back, he suddenly began to describe Manderley. Not of his life but of the glow of the setting sun, the daffodils in bloom, the bluebells best enjoyed in the woods.

As he spoke, we were in the Monte Carlo traffic with dusk closing in on us. Soon the enchanting afternoon would

be over and I reached for my gloves in the pocket of the car. My hands closed in on a book which seemed like one of poetry. I could take it and read it he said. I agreed readily just to be able to carry with me some possession of his.

"I shan't be seeing you for dinner," he said as I hopped out of the car. "I am out for dinner, but thank you for today." I entered the hotel like a despairing child whose treat is over and dreaded the rest of the day that lay ahead. I sat in the lounge and ordered tea. Then I picked the book of poems and began to read one.

I kept the book away and thought of the hill and the distance of half the length of the car and the two thousand feet drop and what had brought it all on. I pictured him in his valley.

I picked the book again and this time it opened at the title page, with the dedication, 'Max—from Rebecca. 17 May.'

This was written in a slanting hand and the R stood out black and strong.

I put the book away. Mrs. Van Hopper was telling me at the table yesterday, "An appalling tragedy. They say he never talks about it. She was drowned in the bay near Manderley."

Max
from
Rebecca

Chapter 5

Memories in a Bottle

No matter what the poets say, but I am glad that the fever of first love can happen only once. The age when we are twenty-one is an age of cowardice. Little fears with no foundation tingle us all the time.

Propped against her pillows, with the illness almost gone and with an irritability that comes with it, Mrs. Van Hopper asked, “What have you been doing this morning?”

I reached for the pack of cards at the bedside drawer and said, “I have been playing tennis with the professional.” Even as I said it, I panicked wondering what if the professional were to come up to the suite?

Shuffling the cards like an inveterate player, shaking them in three and then snapping the backs, she said, “The trouble is, with me laid up in bed, there isn’t much for you to do. Hope your tennis improves, it will be useful to you later. Do you serve underhand?”

I thought to myself how ironic, that I was serving underhand. I don't know why I didn't tell her that every morning I drove with Maxim de Winter and then had lunch with him in the restaurant.

I have forgotten much of Monte Carlo, where we went on our morning drives or what we spoke; all I remember is running down the stairs, too impatient to wait for the lift, brushing past the swing doors and into the car. He would be parked, reading his newspaper. Then, as I sat, he would toss the paper on the back seat and ask, "How is my friend this morning and where does she want to go?"

It didn't matter to me whether we drove around in circles. I was in the flushed world of first love, putting on his coat when the wind was cold, the wind blowing my dull, lanky hair. What he said or didn't say didn't matter at all and my only foe was the clock on the dashboard when it would soon be time to return to the hotel. We passed numerous villages but all those hamlets were but a blur.

Wistfully I said, "I wish there was an invention where our memories could be bottled like a perfume. Then when we wanted, we could uncork the bottle and live that moment again."

"What memories of your young life would you want to uncork?" he asked, continuing to drive. He didn't seem to be teasing me and I floundered and said, "This very

moment which I never want to forget."

"Is that a compliment for me or for my driving?" he laughed like a mocking brother and I realized how the gulf between us widened more because of his very kindness.

Throwing caution to the wind, I said, "I wish I were a lady of thirty-six wearing black satin and a string of pearls."

"If you were, you would not be in the car with me," he said, "and will you stop biting those nails, they are horrid enough already."

"You might think I am impolite and discourteous but why do you choose me for your charity? Why do you ask me to come out with you every day?"

"Because," he said, "you are not a lady of thirty-six wearing black satin and a string of pearls."

"All that is fine," I said, "but you know everything about me, not that there is much, except people dying, and I know nothing of you than what I did when we first met."

"And what did you know then?"

"That you lived at Manderley and you had lost your wife." The forbidden word had at last been said. I saw before the curious inscription R in a slanting hand in the book of poems. I felt sick at heart thinking he might now never forgive me and this will be the end of us. The silence between us stretched to minutes and minutes to miles.

I suddenly began to imagine about how tomorrow I will be back with Mrs. Van Hopper and the gentleman by my side will pack and leave. I was so consumed by my thoughts that I did not realize that he had parked the car by the side of the road. He wore a somber expression. Without his hat and with a scarf round his neck he looked like a medieval figure. The friend I knew or the brother who chided me for biting my nails was gone. Then, like a stranger, he turned towards me and spoke.

"A little while ago you said that you wanted to bottle all your memories, I, on the other hand, want to erase all the memories of my past for they are bitter. A year ago, something dreadful happened and I want to forget my existence until then. When Mrs. Van Hopper asked why I had come to Monte Carlo it was to put a stopper on those memories. And you want to revive them. But the fragrance of the past can be overpowering and sometimes all consuming. The other day atop the hill, I was there a few years ago with my wife. You asked me if it was the same, yes, it was, however, I am grateful that this time it was peculiarly impersonal. You have blotted out the past for me much more than the bright lights of Monte Carlo. Had it not been for you I would have moved onto Italy and Greece and further. Your idea of charity and kindness is insane. I want you because I want you and your company and if you don't believe me then leave my car and find your way home."

I sat still and he asked "What are you going to do?" I could feel the tears prickle behind me eyes and had I been younger I possibly would have cried. I made a sorry figure and said, "I want to go home."

We covered the distance too easily and rapidly and the countryside seemed to watch us with heartless eyes. The grown-up pride in me was gone and my cheeks were stained with tears. I didn't know whether he saw me crying for I didn't reach for a handkerchief and he tossed his onto my lap. He took my hand in his and kissed it.

I thought how all the pretty heroines looked when crying and I, in contrast, was a sight with red eyes and a blotched face. What a miserable finish to the day and the rest of it lay ahead with Mrs. Van Hopper's room strewn with half folded papers, thumped up pillows, crumpled sheets, the dusty table and she would make me play Bezique with the energy of a convalescent, because the nurse was going out. He, on the other hand, would drop me and go somewhere with his memories and the chasm between us now lay wider. I forgot my pride and blew into his handkerchief. "To hell with this," he suddenly said and pulled me beside him and out his arm around my shoulder.

"You are young enough to be my daughter and I don't know how to deal with you."

"Forget everything I said to you this morning, let's not ever think of it and please call me Maxim as my family does, we have been very formal with each other." He took my hat and threw it over the back seat and kissed the top of my head and said, "Promise me, you will never wear black satin again." I smiled, he laughed and the morning was happy again.

Later that evening, while playing Bezique, Mrs. Van Hopper asked, "Is Max de Winter still in the hotel?" I hesitated, lost my nerve for a bit, and then said, "Yes, I believe so; he comes into the restaurant for his meals." Someone has said something to her, I thought but she continued to put the cards into the box.

"I never saw her but they say, she was beautiful, gorgeously turned out, brilliant in every way and gave marvelous parties," she said.

Her visitors started coming in. I changed the records on the gramophone, made a little conversation, and handed them their drinks but all the while my mind was afloat. There was a phantom that had taken shape in my mind—what must she have been like?

And I had to call him Maxim.

Chapter 6

Mrs. Max de Winter

Packing up. A flutter in the belly. A nagging worry of what could be left behind. A mechanical motion of opening and closing of drawers and wardrobes. Even after living off suitcases I hate it, for it gives me a sense of sadness. No matter that the room or the furniture doesn't belong to us. As far as we live in it, we leave a certain something of ourselves behind, for every moment is a memory, it is an experience.

There was an air of finality as the locks snapped shut. The room wore an empty look. It was yesterday while pouring her coffee at breakfast that she flung a letter at me, "Helen is sailing for New York because little Nancy has a threatened appendix. We are going too, anyway, I am sick of Europe. How do you like the idea of seeing New York?"

Something of my displeasure must have shown on my face for she immediately said, "What an odd child you are! Girls in your position with no money could have so much fun and you needn't be at my beck and call as you are here."

"I have gotten used to it," I said lamely.

"Well, you will have to get used to New York too. Now we have to catch that boat of Helen's and see about our passage immediately. Run down and make that clerk show some efficiency, you will be so busy today that you won't have the time to miss anything."

I could not go down immediately. I went to the bathroom and sat down and held my head in my hands. It had finally come, the time to part. Tomorrow evening I will be in a train clutching her jewel case and her rug.

Perhaps I should say goodbye in the lounge with a furtive remark or two, whereas my yearning heart would scream, "I love you so much. I am terribly unhappy." Sitting in the bathroom on the cork mat I was imagining all the possible goodbyes and then our journey, and the arrival in New York, the piercing voice of Helen—a narrower version of her mother—and Nancy, the horrid little child. I would want to be alone with my thoughts, as I was now, behind the door of the bathroom. Just then, she came and rattled on the door, "What are you doing?"

"Sorry, coming now," I said and made a few pretenses

of having used the bathroom.

With a curious glance, she said, "You have been in for a time. You cannot afford to dream this morning, there is much to do."

I was certain that in a few weeks he would go to Manderley where a great pile of letters would be waiting for him. Mine would be one and he would reply in a hurry before his Sunday lunch. Then no more until Christmas.

I went down. The reception clerk said that it was too bad that we were leaving tomorrow since the ballet would start next week. I dragged myself back from thoughts of Manderley.

That afternoon Mrs. Van Hopper lunched at the restaurant for the first time since her influenza. I had a pain in the pit of my stomach that a waiter might be indiscreet and ask if Monsieur will be dining with me tonight. He said nothing. And I knew that he was at Cannes today.

The day was spent in packing and in the evening, people came to say good-bye. She went to bed early. Even then I had not met him. At 9:30 I went down on the pretext of getting luggage labels and still he was not there. The loathsome clerk smiled and said, "If you are looking for Mr. de Winter he is not going to be back from Cannes until midnight, we had a message from him."

"I need a packet of luggage labels," I said but he was not to be deceived.

I cried that night, deep into the pillow. A throbbing head and swollen eyes and the anxiety of hiding it all the next morning with a dash of powder, a dab of eau de cologne. I opened the windows wide and the fresh air and bright sun held a promise.

"You are not coming down with a cold? Are you?" she asked me at breakfast.

"No," I said.

She grumbled that she hated to hang around once she was packed and that we ought to have decided on an earlier train. "We could get it if we tried and then have more time in Paris. Wire Helen not to meet us. Go down to the office and see if our reservations can be changed."

"Yes," I said as I went into my room to change, my indifference towards Mrs. Van Hopper turning into hatred. Because she was bored, she had taken my last half hour away from me.

I threw all diffidence and restraint away and ran along the passage, climbed the stairs three at a time and hammered breathlessly at room 148.

"Come in," he shouted. I lost my nerve and repented

my decision and wondered if he would still be in bed after arriving late last night. He was shaving by the open window.

"What do you want? Is something the matter?" he asked.

"I have come to say good-bye, we are leaving."

He stared at me and said, "Shut the door. What on earth are you saying?"

The words tumbled out, "We were to leave by a later train but she wants to catch the earlier one and I was afraid I won't see you again. I wanted to see you before leaving and say thank you."

"Why didn't you say anything earlier?" he said.

"She decided yesterday in a hurry. Her daughter sails for New York and we are going with her. And I don't want to go, I will be miserable."

"Why go then?"

"I have to! I work for a salary and I can't afford to leave her."

"Sit down," he said taking the soap off his face, "I'll dress in the bathroom and be ready in five minutes."

I sat on the bed and bit my nails in anxiety. His room was typical of a man, with things strewn around, quite untidy and impersonal. I looked around for a photograph but there were none.

As promised, he was ready in five minutes and asked me to come to the terrace as he ate his breakfast.

"I haven't got the time. I am supposed to be at the office to change my reservation."

"Never mind that, I want to talk to you."

We took the lift to the terrace where he ordered his breakfast.

"Mrs. Van Hopper is bored of Monte Carlo and wants to go home," he said, "and so do I. She will go to New York; I will go to Manderley. Which would you prefer? Take your pick."

"Don't make a joke of it, I will say good-bye and leave now and see to those tickets," I said.

"I am usually ill-tempered early in the morning, and this is no joke. I repeat, you either go to America with Mrs. Van Hopper or come home to Manderley with me."

"Do you want me as your secretary or something?"

"No, my little fool, I am asking you to marry me and be my wife."

I waited for the waiter to serve breakfast and leave the table, "You don't understand, men like you do not marry people like me."

"What the hell does that mean?"

"I don't really know. For one, I don't belong to your

kind of world."

"And what world is that?"

"Well, Manderley, you know what I mean."

"You are just as ignorant and foolish as Mrs. Van Hopper. I am to decide whether you belong to Manderley or not. And you believe that I ask this of you as charity just as I did when driving you around. One day," he continued spreading marmalade on his toast, "you will realize that philanthropy is not my strongest attribute. Are you then going to marry me?"

I had had this thought a time or two when we were driving and I imagined other circumstances like when maybe I had nursed him of a delirium and one other time I imagined living at a lodge in the grounds of Manderley and he would visit me and sit by the fire. This sudden talk of marriage left me bewildered. In books men proposed to women kneeling in the moonlight, not at the breakfast table.

"You do not like my suggestion, I see, what a blow to my vanity. I thought you loved me."

"Oh! I do love you, in fact, I love you dreadfully and I cried all night thinking I should never see you again."

He laughed, took my hand in his and said, "When you reach the exalted age of thirty-six which you have been wanting to, I will remind of you of this moment.

What a pity that you must grow up."

I felt a little ashamed and angry at all the confessions that I had made.

"It is settled then, instead of being a companion to Mrs. Van Hopper you will be mine and your duties will also be the same."

As I drummed my fingers on the table not sure of myself, he said, "I know this is not the kind of proposal you expected, we in a conservatory, you in a white frock, violins playing; nevertheless, I will make it up by taking you to Venice for our honeymoon but we must return soon for I want to show Manderley to you." My mind ran riot to the picture postcard I had bought as a child. Was it a premonition?

I imagined myself as Mrs. de Winter and the life that would be mine; being introduced to people or inviting them over to Manderley.

I was jolted out of my reverie when he said the tangerine was sour and folding his napkin casually asked if I would break the news to Mrs. Van Hopper or should he. My goodness, how casual he was whereas for me it was a bombshell. As we got up from the table, I thought he would perhaps tell the waiter, "Won't you congratulate us, we are to be married," but he said nothing and we left the terrace.

"You tell her, she will be very angry," I said.

As we went up, he asked, "Does forty-two seem very old to you?"

"Oh no! I don't like young men," I said quickly.

"How would you know when you haven't known any?"

At the door to the suite he suggested that it would be better if he confronted her alone and then asked if it were alright for us to be married soon.

"You don't need a trousseau or anything like that, do you? The whole thing can easily be arranged with a license and we can be off to Venice or wherever else you might fancy."

"No church? No bridesmaids and the bride in white? No friends or relatives?" I asked.

"I had that kind of wedding before."

"Yes, of course," I said. "I thought for a minute, that possibly we would be married at home. Naturally, I don't expect a church or people." And with a cheery smile I said, "It will be fun."

We opened the door and were in the passage of the suite. "Is that you?" she called out. "Where have you been? I have called the office thrice and they haven't seen you."

"I am afraid it has all been my fault," he said closing the door behind him as I heard her gasp with surprise.

And then I waited in my little bedroom, hugging my

knees by the window seat, waiting patiently, wondering what conversation was taking place, much like relatives wait at the ante room of a doctor's clinic for a verdict.

He had not mentioned love, maybe it was all very hurried. Do young men talk and blabber of love? What was it like with Rebecca? Oh! Rebecca, Satan, I must forever push those thoughts away. The book of poems was lying by my side. I should just pack it away, not open it; he had forgotten he had lent it to me. The title page, "Max from Rebecca," fell open and I tore it neatly, looking over my shoulder like a criminal.

"Oh, how much longer were they going to be?"

I looked at the fragments in the waste paper basket, took a match and set fire to them. The letter R was the last to go, twisting in the flame. I washed my hands and came out with a feeling of being new and clean, like when the calendar says January the 1st.

The door opened and he said, "All is well. Go and meet her. She was shocked at first but is beginning to recover. I will go to the office and ensure she gets the train."

I went into the room. She was smoking by the window and said, "Well, you have been a double-time worker. Still waters certainly run deep in your case. It was a lucky thing I had influenza. Tennis lessons, Huh?! You could have told me."

"I am sorry," I said.

She ran her eyes up and down scrutinizing me, "And he wants to marry you in a few days. You do realize he is much older than you, don't you?

And he has not asked me to the wedding."

"He doesn't want anybody," I said.

"Hmm..., I suppose you know your mind and you know life won't be easy for you. You will be mistress of Manderley. Your work cut out for you. You scarcely can string two sentences together with my bridge friends, what are you going to say to his friends. The parties at Manderley were famous when she was alive. Anyway, I wish you well but I do think you are making a big mistake."

Her barbed words didn't matter. When I burnt the fragments, a fresh confidence came over me. I grudged the time I had spent with her and taken her money and I was glad she was going. Soon Max and I would be in the dining room planning our future and talking of love.

She continued to look at me through the looking glass and I thought she would finally say a kind word and wish me well. Instead she said, "You know that he is marrying you not for love, don't you? The empty house got to him and he even admitted it to me. He just can't live there alone anymore..."

Chapter 7

Mrs. de Winter Comes to Manderley

We arrived at Manderley in early May and as Maxim said, with the first swallows and bluebells. It would be the best time of year before the full onslaught of summer. When we left London in the morning it was raining and I looked upon it as a bit of an ill-omen and it made me silent. But as we drove further, Maxim said, "This is London rain and by the time we reach Manderley, the sun will be shining for you." He was right, because as we drove, the clouds left us at Exeter.

I, a bride of seven weeks, unsuitably dressed as always, was wearing a stockinette frock, an ill-fitting mackintosh, clutching a pair of gauntlet gloves and carrying a large hand bag.

I thought how easy it would be for Maxim to go back to his own familiar home, pick the mail from the table, and ring a bell for tea. However, he could not fathom my nervousness. He held my hand and said, "I expect you will want your tea," as we had expected to arrive at five o'clock in time for it.

The moment was upon me and I wished I could delay it.

"Two miles to go. Do you see the green belt of trees on the brow of the hill sloping to the valley and the sea beyond? Manderley lies in there," he said. Panic and an uneasy feeling gripped me leaving behind the seven weeks I had had as a happy bride. I was like a child on her first day of school. I wouldn't know my right hand from my left and which fork to use at dinner.

"Here we are," he said with triumph and excitement.

The road curved, before us were two iron gates which opened to a long drive. A child came darting from the back looking curiously. "You must not mind the curiosity," he said taking my hand, kissing it and guessing that I was shy. "They have probably not spoken of anything else for a week."

"Just be yourself and they will adore you. You don't have to worry about the house. Mrs. Danvers does everything. She'll be stiff with you at first but that's her manner and do not let it bother you."

He was pointing to some shrubs and my mind was on the picture post card which would have done nicely for my

album and instead the mansion on the picture was to be my home now. I envied the smile on Maxim's face and his ease; he was happy to be home.

The gates had shut with a crash behind us and the driveway was not as I had imagined. It was not a neat broad path of gravel flanked by turf. Instead, there were twists and turns, like a serpent. The branches of the trees intermingled above us making an archway like the roof of a church. It was all very still and silent and even the sun found it difficult to penetrate the branches.

The drive went on and on giving me an edgy feeling. Suddenly, there was a burst of bright red color flanking us and they were the rhododendrons. He smiled and asked if I had liked them and I said "yes" a little breathlessly.

And ahead of us lay the beautiful, exquisite Manderley, the way it was on my picture post card.

I saw through a window that there were a lot of people in the hall. "Damn that woman, she knows I didn't want that sort of thing."

"Who are these people?"

"Mrs. Danvers has collected all the staff from the house and estate to welcome us. But I will handle it."

The butler, Frith, who was a kind old man came to help us out and enquired after us.

We went up the stairs: Frith, the footman, Maxim and I. "This won't take long," he said, "and then we can have tea."

I stood at the threshold as I took it all in, the great stone hall, the wide doors to the library, a gorgeous staircase leading to the minstrels' gallery. A sea of faces were gaping at us and from among them emerged a woman dressed in black with prominent cheek bones and great hollow eyes. Her face was parchment white.

Maxim introduced her to me as Mrs. Danvers. She gave a little rehearsed speech saying that she welcomed me. Her hollow eyes were staring into mine and her handshake was cold and lifeless just like her words. I dropped my gloves in nervousness and when she picked them up, she gave me a scornful smile, considering me to be ill-bred.

Maxim thanked everyone on our behalf and we were finally alone again in the library for tea. Two cocker spaniels came to greet us; Jasper, the younger, put his nose into my hand and I caressed his silken ears. The library was a comfortable room, with books lined against the wall.

Soon tea was brought, a little ritual performed by Frith and the footman. I played with two dripping crumpets and cake while Maxim looked at his mail and smiled at me when he looked up. Driving through France and Italy I only knew

of a carefree laughing gentleman whom I loved terribly. Little did I think of his responsibilities back home or what his everyday life would be like.

My thoughts were disturbed by Frith coming to clear the tea and ask me, "Would you like to see your room, madam? Mrs. Danvers was wondering."

Maxim, glancing up from his letters, asked Frith what job they had done of the east wing.

"Have you been making changes?" I asked.

"Just a few my dear, I thought we would use the east wing as it is more cheerful and airy. It overlooks the rose garden. My mother used it for visitors during her time. Why don't you have a look and make friends with Mrs. Danvers while I finish here and follow you?"

I got up with all my nervousness returning and walked through the large hall, which Frith explained, served as a banqueting hall in the old days. "The public are admitted here once a week," he said.

A stern figure dressed in black, watching me with intent eyes was waiting for me at the end of the stairs. "Sorry to keep you waiting," I said lamely. To which she replied, "It is for you to take your time and me to carry out your orders."

We went through a series of doors and stairs and then she flung open a door and allowed me to pass. There was

a little sitting room furnished with a sofa, chairs and a writing desk, which opened to a huge double bedroom and beyond that, the bathroom. The rose garden lay below and then a smooth grass bank that led to the woods.

"You can't see the sea from here, then?" I asked. "I like the sea."

"No, not from here." She replied in a peculiar way. "From this wing you would not know that there is a sea nearby."

I asked if this room was refurbished for us and whether it was used as his bedroom originally.

"No, never used a room here," she said.

All my things were unpacked and Mrs. Danvers said that Alice, the housemaid, would be mine until someone was found for me.

"Oh, I am sure Alice will do well," I said and received the same expression of derision that I had when I had dropped my gloves.

"Ladies in your position do need a maid, Madam, and this won't do for long."

"Well then, perhaps, a young girl who would like to train," I said.

"As you wish, Madam," she said continuing to wait sternly, while I wished she would leave.

I continued my efforts and asked if she had been at Manderley longer than anyone else. She said that she had come with the first Mrs. de Winter, her voice turning even harsher, and that Frith had been here since Max was a little boy.

I could see that she hated me and that there was nastiness and loathing in her demeanor.

"Mrs. Danvers, I hope we can be friends. You will have to be a little patient with me as this sort of a life is new to me. You may continue to run the house as you have been doing," I said wanting to make a fresh attempt.

"I have been in-charge of the house for a year now and of course when the first Mrs. de Winter was alive there was a lot of entertaining and parties. I handled everything but she did like to supervise. The rooms in the west wing are larger and beautiful. The room overlooking the sea, was their bedroom."

Thank goodness I saw a shadow and Maxim entered. "I always thought this was a lovely room; wasted on guests. Thank you Mrs. Danvers for making a success of it," he said.

"There is something about this room; so peaceful and happy and who could tell that the sea was only five minute from here."

He further said, "How did you get on with Mrs Danvers?"

"She seemed a bit stiff," I said.

"Don't mind her, if she does make a nuisance, we will find a replacement."

"It is natural for her to resent me as she was used to looking after a man and a house alone."

"Resent you?! Why on earth? Anyway, enough of her, let's forget her and come along as I show you a little more of Manderley."

Maxim said it was too late to change for dinner and I was glad to have been spared the scrutiny of Mrs. Danvers and have Alice ask me what I should wear. We ate in the austere dining room laughing and talking of our escapades and Frith and the footman were like the waiters in Italy and France.

After dinner, we retired into the library where the warmth of the fire was welcoming. He reached for his paper. All the while a shiver ran down me to think that whatever I was doing and whatever I was touching had all once belonged to Rebecca.

Chapter 8

The Morning After...

Life at Manderley was orderly and planned. At nine o'clock, when I came down for breakfast, Maxim was already peeling his fruit ready for the morning. "Don't mind my rushing off, a place like Manderley is not easy to run. We help ourselves to breakfast. Tea and hot dishes are on the side-board."

"And by the way," he continued as I mumbled a few excuses for being late, "I don't have many relations to impose upon you but my sister Beatrice and her husband Giles will join us for lunch. I suppose they are curious to see you and you will like Beatrice; she just says whatever she thinks. I would have liked to show the gardens to you but I have to see my estate agent Crawley, who will also join us for lunch. Hope you don't mind that. I expect you will be able to amuse yourself this morning."

"Of course," I said feeling anxious about the arrival of

the guests this afternoon. After Maxim had left, I looked around at all the food laid out and wondered where all the scrambled eggs and bacon and fish and porridge went. I dare not ask.

I took a boiled egg and lingered over it until when Frith appeared. I realized it was past ten. I got up hurriedly and made an apology which I suppose was not the right thing to do and stumbled out of the door. My lack of poise and grace were perhaps being spoken about as I heard murmurs and giggles as I crossed the hall and wondered whether I was being laughed at.

I went to the library. The room was chilly and I began to look for a match to light the fire. I could go to my room but that would not be appropriate so I waited for the dining room to be cleared so I could get one from there.

Just as I was trying to furtively pocket a box of matches Frith came in and asked if I wanted something. Embarrassed, I said, "A box of matches," and he immediately gave one to me and cigarettes. Now that was another awkward thing for, I did not smoke.

"No Frith, I just wanted the fire in the library to be li as it is rather cold."

"The fire in the library is usually lit only in the afternoon, Madam, but if you would like I will give order

to have it done. Mrs. de Winter always used the morning room where there is a fire in the morning and did all her correspondence and telephoning from there. You may reach Mrs. Danvers on the house telephone. There are pens, writing paper and ink in there," he explained.

"Thank you," I said and made a brave attempt at finding the room. Frith was watching of course. "You go through the drawing room," he said directing me through a maze of stairs and rooms.

I walked through the long drawing room which had all the trappings of a museum. I finally turned in to the morning room. The dogs were sitting by the fire and I was glad to see them. The window overlooked the blood red and blooming rhododendrons.

This was a woman's room with all the best treasures of Manderley. The rhododendrons lay in a bowl on the mantelpiece. The writing table was beautiful and the pigeon holes were docketed, 'letters unanswered,' 'household,' 'estate' and so on. And then the scrawling pointed handwriting startled me for I had not seen it since the day that I had set that page on fire.

I opened a drawer and in it I found a book, *Guests at Manderley*, where every detail of every guest had been noted including what they had eaten and where they had slept. There was notepaper of the house with the crest and the address and ivory white visiting cards that read, 'Mrs. de Winter,' and 'Manderley' at the corner. I felt like a trespasser and when the telephone rang suddenly, I was startled and answering it with trembling hands, asked, "Who is it? What do you want?"

"Mrs. de Winter? Mrs. de Winter…" came a voice.

"I am afraid you have made a mistake; Mrs. de Winter has been dead for over a year."

"It's Mrs. Danvers, Madam," she said and I stared foolishly into the mouthpiece and said, "Sorry, I was alarmed by the telephone."

"I am sorry Madam to have bothered you but I was wondering if you would like to see me and whether you approve of the menu for today? You will find the menu on the blotter beside you."

"Oh, I am sure it is fine, Mrs. Danvers," I said. She continued to prod me asking if I needed changes and what sauce I would prefer as Mrs. de Winter was very particular about her sauces.

"I think we better have what you usually have," I said.

"Mrs. de Winter would have preferred the wine sauce."

"Then we will have the same."

"Robert will come for your letters and stamp them as the post leaves midday," and then, there was a click.

I felt so idle compared to the lady who occupied my position before me. Who would she have written to? Dressmakers? Hair dressers? Who should I write to? Ironically, I took a notepaper and pen and wrote to the lady I despised and whom I would never see again. "Dear Mrs. Van Hopper," I began, enquiring after her voyage, her daughter and the weather in New York.

Then I heard the sound of a car and panic gripped me for I knew Beatrice and her husband had arrived and Maxim was not home yet. I wanted to hide but Frith was bringing them in through the garden knowing I was in the morning room. I thought I should go to my room and sit there until lunch time when I would be obliged to come down out of good manners.

I dashed into the big drawing room and into a door on the left. I knew I was being senseless but I could not help myself. I lost my bearings and came to a corridor I had not seen before and found it was very dark and quiet. It looked oppressively empty and there was no one around.

I opened a door and found it in complete darkness, smelling musty, furniture as if covered in dust sheets. I shut the door and went uncertainly along the corridor. I reached an alcove where a broad window gave me light and upon looking down, I saw that the grass lawns stretched to the

sea. The bright green sea appeared to be so close. I knew then that I was standing in the west wing of the house. There was an unnerving feeling about the sea creeping upon the house and I was happy that my rooms were in the east wing, the rose garden was better than the sea.

I was about to go down when I heard a door behind me click and standing there was Mrs. Danvers. I explained that I had lost my way and she asked me with a hint of anger if I had gone into any of the rooms and like a guilty child, I said that I had only opened a door and didn't mean to disturb anything.

"You have only to tell me if you would like to see the rooms and I shall show them to you," she said. "Mrs. Lacy and Major Lacy have been here some time," she said and waited like a black guard to see where I was going.

Maxim was back and when I opened the door to the morning room, a sea of faces greeted me and Maxim made quick introductions — Beatrice, Giles and Frank Crawley.

Beatrice was tall, broad-shouldered, quite like Maxim but not as smart as I had imagined her to be, a more homely sort of person; Giles had genial eyes behind horn rimmed glasses; and Frank Crawley was a thin man with a prominent Adam's apple. When he saw me he seemed relieved and I wondered why?

Beatrice shook hands with me firmly and said I wasn't what she had expected. She looked me up and down but I appreciated her straightforwardness unlike Mrs. Danvers' maliciousness.

"You are looking good, young man!"

"Gosh! Six months ago we thought you were going in for a breakdown," and turning towards me she continued, "and I guess, we have you to thank for it."

I could tell that Maxim was trying to get a hold on his temper. Then, they argued about their dogs. There was a strain on the siblings as they argued. It was discomfiting.

They spoke of hunting and riding and when I said I did neither they were horrified at how I would pass my time. Maxim said that I did paint but that didn't satisfy them for that could be done when one was bound indoors like on a wet day and didn't offer fresh air or exercise. I said I would bathe in the warmer climes.

"Not everyone is a fresh air monster like you Beatrice."

"You are just happy walking about Manderley," she said. "Oh, I like walking too," I interjected. "And I can bathe when it is warmer."

"The bay is safe, isn't it, with not very strong currents?" I asked and an uncanny silence fell upon the room and I knew instantly, my mistake.

"Jasper could do with a swim to get that fat off," Beatrice said finally and broke the silence. At long last, Frith announced lunch and Beatrice and I walked together ahead of the others. "I congratulate you on his looks," she said. "Although we fight a lot, I am devoted to Maxim and we were very worried about him this time last year. Of course, you do know the whole story." We entered the dining room and I thought to myself that I knew nothing of it.

Throughout lunch Frank Crawley made easy conversation with me and at the end of it I looked at Maxim to see if I was to do anything. Finally, I moved my chair and, in the bargain, upset Giles's glass of port and Maxim said irritably that Frith would clear up and that Beatrice and I should take a walk around the garden. "She has barely seen the place," he added. The lunch, I could see, was such a strain on Maxim and me.

Beatrice asked what I was doing in the South of France and I told her of Mrs. Van Hopper. Beatrice said quite frankly that they expected I would be something of a social butterfly but when I walked into the morning room she could have been knocked down by a feather. We both laughed and she continued, "We are very different; I show everything on my face but Maxim, never."

"Don't mind my saying it but you must do something

about your hair and didn't Maxim buy you clothes in London. Does he like your hair?"

"He hasn't said anything."

"Oh, well, he must have changed," she said.

"How do you get on with Mrs. Danvers?" she asked next. "Don't let her ever frighten you although I would not want anything to do with her and she is rather civil with me. She might make things unpleasant for you initially but she will get over her jealousy and resentment."

"Why is she jealous? And why would she resent me?" I asked.

"I thought you would know and Maxim must have told you, she simply adored Rebecca."

We stroked and patted Jasper who was enjoying the attention. Just then the men came out.

Mr. Crawley thanked me for lunch and said that he should be off and I said that he must come often.

Meanwhile, Robert brought chairs and rugs and we settled down under the chestnut tree. I was wondering how long they would stay for I wanted to be with Maxim alone. Giles soon began to snore and Maxim and Beatrice began speaking of their grandmother.

"We must go see her," Maxim said.

"She's getting gaga," said Beatrice.

I leaned against his arm as he stroked my hand, just like I did with Jasper.

It all seemed so idyllic, the smoke from the chimney, the soft breeze, the sweet scent of magnolia, the distant murmur of the sea — exactly what I hoped life at Manderley would be. I wanted to cherish these moments and keep them close.

Soon Beatrice and Giles were saying their goodbyes and moving to their car when Maxim asked if they had seen the east wing. I insisted that they should come up and do so, it wouldn't take long. Beatrice wondered if the dinghy room she had known of should look as it did now, overlooking the rose garden.

The men went down and Beatrice powdered her nose.

"We must give a wedding present to you."

"You must not bother," I said.

"I would not grudge your wedding present to you although we were not invited," Beatrice said.

"I hope you don't mind but that is how Maxim wanted it."

"Not at all! In fact, very sensible, after all, it wasn't…" and she cut herself off going back on the subject of a wedding present.

She got up from the dressing table asking me if we were

likely to have a lot of people over at Manderley. I said that Maxim hadn't said anything.

"Funny old boy, at one time the house would be chock-a-block, but somehow I can't see you…" and she stopped herself, instead saying, "it is a pity you don't ride or shoot. Do you sail?"

"No, I don't," I said.

"Thank God for that," she said.

"You must come see us if you like, I like it that way, instead of having to send out invitations."

We were at the head of the stairs and Giles asked her to hurry for it was threatening to rain.

She gave a quick peck on my cheek and said as she walked down the stairs, "Sorry if I have asked a lot of questions and been rude, but tact was never my strong point. You see, you are very different from what I expected, very different from Rebecca."

Robert was hurrying across the lawn to bring the chairs in as the sun had vanished behind the clouds and a light drizzle was beginning to fall.

Chapter 9

The Mysterious Cottage

The visit of Beatrice and Giles had put a strain on Maxim and I wondered why. As soon as they left, he asked Robert to fetch a coat and we set out for a walk. He asked me what I thought of Beatrice and I said I liked her very much.

"She does tend to put her foot in her mouth, although she is a very nice person," he said, leaving me to wonder where she had blundered.

"What was she saying?" he asked.

"Oh, nothing much, I did most of the talking and she just said I wasn't what she expected."

"Well, what did she expect?"

"Someone more sophisticated, smarter, a social butterfly."

"Beatrice can sometimes be quite unintelligent," he said.

"Do you like my hair?" I asked.

"Your hair? Of course, I do. Why do you ask?"

"Oh, nothing, I just wondered," I said.

We came to a clearing in the woods and there were two paths. Jasper automatically took the one on the right but Maxim called him back; nonetheless, he stood there wagging his tail, not wanting to come back.

I asked Maxim why he wanted to go that way and he explained that there is a cove there where a boat was kept and Jasper was used to it.

We continued on the left-hand path and came upon a valley. "This is the valley I told you of, the rain will bring out the scent of the azaleas," Maxim said, seeming happy, with his old cheerful self back. He then spoke of Frank Crawley who he said was a thorough gentleman and totally devoted to Manderley. I thought how like Italy this easy camaraderie was.

"There, take a look at that," Maxim said, "we call it the Happy Valley." It was splendidly breathtaking as we stood on the slope of a wooded hill and before us, the path wound to a valley beside a running stream. Beautiful azaleas and white and gold rhododendrons flanked the path making the air heady with their fragrance.

The sounds of the stream and falling rain were

interjected by those of the singing birds and the magical spell of the Happy Valley fell upon me. This is the Manderley I would always cherish and remember.

Maxim smiled, watching me perplexed and wondrous all at once. "It is a shock, isn't it?" he asked me. "No one guesses it for the contrast is so sudden." He flung a stone across the beach for, Jasper to go and fetch. The earlier spell was broken and we were ourselves again playing along on the beach.

Suddenly, we discovered that Jasper was nowhere. We called out to him, "Jasper! Jasper!"

"If he had fallen, we would have seen him," he said.

"Perhaps he has gone back to the Happy Valley," I said.

Then, to the right of the beach, beyond the rocks, we heard a sharp bark. I scrambled up the slippery rocks to find Jasper while Maxim asked me in a hard voice to get back.

As I climbed and slipped on the rocks finding my way towards Jasper, Maxim got irritable and asked me to leave him alone. I wondered why Maxim was being so heartless.

I came up the big boulder and was surprised to find another cove just like the one we were at, except a bit wider. There was small stone breakwater thrown across the cove and behind it was small natural harbor. There was a buoy anchored but no boat. At the periphery of the woods, there was a low building like a cottage cum boat house, built from the same stone as the breakwater.

There was a man on the beach who seemed like a fisherman in long boots. Jasper ran around him in circles but he took no notice of him. Maxim was nowhere to be seen. I realized that the man had a toothless grin, a red, wet mouth and small slit eyes like those of an idiot.

He greeted me and said the weather was no good this afternoon.

Jasper was in an exasperating mood and not wanting to come with me so I asked the old man for a string; instead, he kept saying there were no shells. I went to the cottage to look for a string and although the windows were boarded up, the latch opened with only a click. Instead of finding a dusty boat house with ropes and oars, I found a fully furnished cottage. There was a table, chairs, book shelves, a bed and dresser with china on it that had fungus, and for a while I thought the old man lived there but soon discovered that it was not inhabited. The air inside was musty, damp and oppressive and I wanted to escape the place quickly.

As I looked for the string, I chanced upon another door and fearful of what I might discover, I crept in and found the typical boat house stuff in there along with a ball of twine and a knife, with which I cut the string.

When I came out, the man had stopped the digging.

"She don't go in there now," he said. "She's gone in the sea, ain't she? She won't come back no more."

"No, no," I said.

"I never said nothing, did I?" he asked.

"No, of course not, don't worry," I said, and he continued with his digging. I tied the string around Jasper's collar.

Maxim was waiting for me by the side of the rocks. "I am sorry, Jasper would just not come," I said apologetically. He turned brusquely and walked towards the woods and I asked why we were not going back over the rocks.

"What's the point? We're here now," he said momentarily, as we went up a path through the woods.

"Who was that man?" I asked.

"Ben, harmless devil," he answered. "His father was one of the keepers. Where did you get the string?"

"I found it in the cottage."

Maxim seemed annoyed that the cottage door was open.

He continued to walk at an incredible pace. The path was steep with rain trickling down my coat and legs. It was dark, much unlike the Happy Valley. Maxim was getting impatient with Jasper, "Come on Jasper, for God's sake Beatrice was right, the dog is very fat."

"We can't keep pace with you," I said irritably, as my legs were aching.

"You should have listened to me instead of running after the dog, he knew his way back, if I had thought otherwise, would I have left him? You are grumbling because you are tired."

"I am not grumbling! Anyone would be tired walking at this pace and I thought you would come behind me for Jasper," I said.

"Why would I exhaust myself after the dog?" he answered.

"You are only trying to find an excuse," I said.

"My good child, what am I to excuse myself of?"

"Oh, I don't know, stop this," I said wearily.

"No, you began it," he continued.

"For not coming over the rocks."

"And why didn't I?" Maxim continued to prod.

"Oh, Maxim how do I know I am not a thought-reader."

"All women say that when they lose an argument. All right, I didn't want to go there and I never want to go to that God-damned cottage. If you had my memories you would think the same. Now you can digest that and I hope it satisfies you," he said with his face white and eyes strained.

"Please Maxim, forget about this silly argument," I pleaded.

"We should have stayed in Italy and never come back to Manderley, how foolish of me," Maxim said.

We finally came to the top of the path and I realized that we were at the turn which Jasper had wanted to take, the one he was familiar with.

When we went into the house, Maxim's face was hard and he ordered Frith to bring in the tea at once. I held back my tears for had Frith seen them they would be spoken of amongst all the servants.

I slowly walked to the library and knelt by the side of his chair and put my face close to his and said that I loved him and could not bear to see him angry or upset.

He held me tight as if reassuring himself, when swiftly, the door opened and in came Frith and Robert to perform the ritual of afternoon tea.

The episode was behind us and I broke a crumpet for the dogs, not hungry myself and too tired and spent. I felt in my pocket for a handkerchief. It had fallen out of the mackintosh I had worn. It had the tall R monogrammed with de W. As I wiped my fingers, I noticed a dull scent about it. The scent was familiar and it struck me that it was the same as the crumpled white petals of the azaleas in the Happy Valley.

Chapter 10

"So Different from Rebecca..."

The weather, as was usual in the west country, stayed wet and cold for a week and we did not go down to the beach again. I know why some people do not like the sea, it can be quite intimidating with its somber notes and sounds. The memory of everything that day left me utterly disturbed.

My going down that bay had opened a raw wound and although he had recovered and things seemed quite the same, I lived in fear that any mention of the sea should bring that look back into Maxim's eyes.

We were called upon, of course, by people in the county who said that they must pay their respects to the new bride and I feared perpetually that I might say something not meant to be discussed. It haunted me to know that on their way home like Beatrice said, they would say, "She is so different from Rebecca."

I had to return these calls and if Maxim was not with me, I had to brave the formality alone. I was asked, "Will you be entertaining much? The house used to be full in those days." And I would say, "Maxim has not mentioned anything."

It was in the neighboring cathedral town that the wife of the bishop asked me, "Will your husband revive the Manderley Fancy Dress ball? Such a lovely sight. You must use your influence. I remember the one, two years ago. Manderley so lends itself to anything like that."

I smiled as if I knew what she was speaking of and said I would surely ask Maxim about it.

The bishop's wife went on, "I remember a most charming garden party, where tea was served in the rose garden, she was so clever…" and then she trailed off understanding her faux pas. As the clock chimed four, I performed my goodbye ritual and asked her and her husband to call on us and she said I must be sure to ask Mr. de Winter to revive the fancy-dress ball.

On my way home, I pictured the fancy-dress ball — the throng of people, the laughter and chatter, the long tables of food and Maxim standing at the front of the stairs with his pretty and gracious wife.

I despised all these people who came to see me only to

satisfy their curiosity, more so, glancing down to see if I was to have a baby. They criticized my looks, my clothes, and compared me with Rebecca. I didn't want to see any of them again.

Down the drive to Manderley I saw Frank Crawley walking along it a little distance ahead. I asked the chauffeur to stop and got off the car to walk with him.

"Been paying calls Mrs. de Winter?" he asked.

"Yes, Frank," I said and told him that I had been to see the Bishop's wife who wanted to know when we were going to have a fancy-dress ball? "I did not know we had Fancy Dress dances here, Frank?"

With a hint of hesitation and with a troubled expression he said that it was a big annual affair and people came not only from the county but also from London.

"I suppose Rebecca worked hard for it," I said.

"We all worked very hard," he said.

"I don't suppose I should be any good at organizing these things."

"You will not have to do anything. Just be yourself and look decorative," he said.

"Will you ask Maxim about it?" I said

"Why don't you?" he asked.

"No, I don't want to," I said and told him of our going

to the beach the other day where Jasper kept barking at the idiot.

"You must mean Ben," he said, "you needn't fear him."

"Oh, I didn't fear him, but the cottage seems to lie in ruin."

I asked him what the cottage was used for? I realized he always said 'she,' and never 'Rebecca.'

"It was a boat house," he said, uncomfortable about the conversation and then said that she had converted it and used it a lot, even had moonlight picnics and he had attended one or two of them.

"Why is the buoy in the harbor?" I asked.

"The boat used to be marooned there," he answered.

"Her boat? What happened to it? Was it the one she was sailing in when she was drowned? What size was it? How did it capsize?" It was as if I were possessed and had to go on with my questioning.

"It can be stormy in the bay," he replied.

"Could no one get to her?" I asked.

"No one saw the accident for no one knew she had gone."

"Not even at the house?"

"No, she often went alone and slept at the cottage at night."

"After how long was she found and from where?"

"After two months near Edgecoombe," he said.

"How did they know, after two months?" I continued.

"Maxim went to identify her."

Suddenly, I felt sick and hated myself for doing this.

In a desperate attempt I told him that he must think me a beast to dig all this up but living at Manderley, a life I wasn't used to, overwhelming as it is, makes me wonder if I should have married Maxim at all.

Everyone sees me and thinks, "How different she is from Rebecca."

"Mrs. de Winter," Frank said, "please don't think that way. I am so delighted that you have married Maxim and I am sure you will make a great success of it. You are refreshing and charming and if I hear a word of criticism I will ensure that it is never uttered again."

"Thank you, Frank, but I feel stupid, not knowing how to meet people and I feel lacking in grace, beauty and intelligence as opposed to what must have been earlier," I said in agitation.

"You have qualities of kindness, compassion and modesty, that are more important, and although I am bachelor, I am sure it means more to a man than all the wit and beauty in the world," Frank said. "I am sure if Maxim were to hear of this, he would be very distressed."

"You will not tell him?" I said hurriedly.

"Naturally not. You have been good for him. As Mrs. Lacy said, he did seem on the verge of a breakdown. Please don't let any of us go back into the past, Mrs. de Winter," Frank pleaded.

Frank was a friend and ally and the one who made me very happy.

Before we went in and put an end to this conversation forever, perhaps, I asked Frank to answer one last question truthfully and he said he was afraid that if I put him in a spot, he might not be able to.

Manderley lay before us as I asked, "Was Rebecca very beautiful?'

"Yes," he said," I suppose the most beautiful creature I ever saw."

As the days went by at Manderley, I barely saw Mrs. Danvers and I was grateful that she had employed a maid, Clarice, for me who unlike Alice, had no alarming standards. She was the daughter of somebody who worked on the estate.

My fear of Mrs. Danvers began to dissipate because I apprehended that it was not me she resented but who I represented. I was the new Mrs. de Winter. Frank had said I must forget about Rebecca but her presence was everywhere in the house.

A large parcel arrived for me one morning and it was the wedding present Beatrice had promised. I had a childish love for presents and tore at the string excitedly and found four large volumes of *A History of Painting*, with a note saying, 'I hope this is the sort of thing you like, Love Beatrice.'

I wondered where to place the books in the morning room, they seemed so out of place among all the delicate things. However, the room was now mine and I decided to place them on top of the desk. The books swayed as I stood back to watch and they toppled over, upsetting a little china cupid. It broke into fragments and like a guilty child, I glanced at the door, swept the pieces away, put them in an envelope and hid them at the back of a drawer.

Maxim laughed when I showed the books to him. "Dear Bee, she never opens a book if she can help it."

The following day Frith hovered around us after bringing coffee into the library after lunch, for he wished to speak to Maxim.

"There has been an unpleasantness between Robert and Mrs. Danvers, Sir, and she has accused him of stealing a valuable from the morning room."

Maxim said it could have been one of the maids but Frith said that no one had been there since Madam yesterday

and the business was rather unpleasant for Robert and him.

When Maxim learnt that it was the china cupid, he said it was worth a lot and he hated servants' rows and that was for me to solve and thus Mrs. Danvers was summoned.

When Frith left to call Mrs. Danvers, I confessed to Maxim that I was the culprit and he asked why I hadn't said anything.

"I am afraid of them Maxim," I said.

Mrs. Danvers entered and Maxim explained that it was me and not Robert who had broken the valuable china. I felt mortified and said, "I am so sorry." It was as if she knew all along that it was me and not Robert and was waiting for me to confess.

"Is it possible to repair the ornament, Madam?" Mrs. Danvers asked with her stern white face and deep eyes.

"I am afraid it has been broken to pieces," I said.

"And where are those pieces?" Maxim asked.

"At the back of a drawer," I replied

Maxim made light of the incident and said, "Send the pieces to London and see if they can be mended. Frith please ask Robert to dry his tears."

"Next time, Madam, if you could tell me personally of course, I will apologize to Robert," she said.

"Yes," said Maxim, "this is the sort of thing a between

maid would do."

"The between-maid at Manderley is not allowed to touch the valuables in the morning room, sir," she said sternly. "When Mrs. de Winter was alive, we did the valuables together."

"Yes, all right," said Maxim dismissing her and the matter.

But after she left, I repeated my apologies to Maxim and stressed on Mrs. Danvers being upset. "She is not the mistress of the house, you are! Stop behaving like a between-maid."

"I do feel like a between-maid that is why I get along with Clarice. I prefer calling on Clarice's mother than people like the Bishop's wife. I can't help being shy Maxim."

"I know that, darling, but at least make an effort to conquer it."

"I try, Maxim, but you are used to this sort of a life, I am not."

"That's nothing to do with it, I hate it too. I am bored but it has to be done in this part of the world," Maxim said.

"It isn't about boredom; it's the way people look me up and down as if I were a prize cow."

"Who does?"

"Everyone around. What a slap in the eye I must be to

them. You knew I was dull, inexperienced and quiet and that is why you married so there wouldn't be any gossip around me."

Maxim threw his paper and, in a fit, got up and said, "What do you mean? What do you know of any gossip here? Who has been talking to you? Why did you say what you did?"

"I – I don't know," I said, frightened of the way he looked at me.

"I wonder if I did the right thing in marrying you? I was selfish and I am not much of a companion to you. You should have married someone more your age than someone half whose life is behind him," he said.

"That's ridiculous," I said hurriedly. "Age doesn't mean a thing; of course, we are companions."

I put my arms around him and said, "You know I love you more than anything else in the world."

"I should never have rushed you, let you think it over."

"There was nothing to think, Maxim, when someone is so in love," I said.

"Are you happy here? I wonder sometimes," he said looking out of the window.

"Of course, I am very happy and I love Manderley and I will call on people every day if I have to," I said.

"Poor lamb, I am not easy to live with."

"Oh, you are very easy Maxim, you don't drink or grumble or smell."

"If you say so, then it's fine," he said smiling.

"Don't you believe so?" I asked.

I heard myself say, "If you are not happy with me, I will go away."

He took my face in his hands and said that if I believed we were happy then let's just leave it at that for he knew nothing of happiness. He kissed the top of my head and moved away.

"Was the cupid in the lumber room?" I asked.

"No, it was a wedding present. Rebecca knew a lot about China."

He had said the word. He was thinking of her I thought and how ironic that a wedding present to me had destroyed a wedding present to her! "Surely, he is reminiscing," I thought.

I continued to polish my nails and asked him what he was thinking.

"Nothing much," he said. He whistled a tune and said, "I was wondering if they had chosen Surrey side to play Middlesex at the Oval."

Chapter 11

Something Fishy

At the end of June, Maxim had to go to London for two days for a public dinner. A man's dinner, something to do with the county. I dreaded his going. As I saw the car disappear down the drive, I was gripped with an unnatural fear. I sat under the chestnut tree all afternoon with a book but it was of no use.

When I saw Robert run across the lawn, I had a sickening feeling, but he came to say that the porter had called from the club to say Mr. de Winter had arrived ten minutes ago. I slapped my book shut with relief. I was hungry now and went to the dining room and stole some biscuits and an apple. I went to the woods to eat them lest one of the servants see me and tell the cook Mrs. de Winter doesn't care for her food and she should go with the complain to Mrs. Danvers.

With my hunger abated and with Maxim away, I felt like a carefree child who runs out to play on a Saturday afternoon. I wiped the crumbs off my mouth and went with Jasper to the Happy Valley.

Jasper once again bounded off towards the forbidden cove and I scrambled up the rocks after him. With the tide out, the sea looked calm and less formidable.

Even the cottage looked less scary and I decided to go in. After all, it was a cottage.

It was dark with cobwebs. Jasper kept barking infuriatingly especially inside the open door of the boat room. I looked in to see who it was. It was Ben and he seemed to be hiding something. It was a fishing line and he looked at me with frightened eyes and said, "You won't put me to the asylum, will you? I done nothing. I never told no one."

"Of course not Ben, no one will put you away but you mustn't take other people's things or go to the cottage again."

"You have angel's eyes," he said. "Not like the other one."

"I don't know what you mean, Ben. No one will put you in an asylum. Good afternoon," I said and made my way back wanting to run and never wanting to come back here again. I was relieved to come into the open lawns and see Manderley and I thought that I would ask Robert to fetch me my tea underneath the chestnut tree. I realized it was not four yet and early for tea.

I then noticed at the turn of the drive behind the rhododendrons that a car had been parked. I wondered whose it could be and if some visitor had come calling. I looked up at the house and noticed that the shutters of one of the windows was open. A man stood at the window and when he saw me, he immediately withdrew and an arm came across to close the window. The arm belonged to Mrs. Danvers because I observed her black sleeve.

Who could it be? It wasn't public day for on that day Frith did the showing and he was out. Besides, the west wing was never open to the public. Even I hadn't seen it. It was odd that if Mrs. Danvers had friends over, it was on a day when Maxim was out. I walked towards the house aware that I might still be watched.

As I entered, I looked for a card on the salver or a cap or stick and knew it was not an official visit. I went into the flower room to wash my hands wanting to avoid meeting them on the staircase or elsewhere. I then went into the morning room and noticed that my knitting which was on the divan had been moved. It was disconcerting that Mrs. Danvers entertained someone in the morning room in our absence. I picked my knitting to walk out when I heard the door to the drawing room open. I stepped back and hid and wondered if Jasper would give me away.

"I suppose she has gone to the library," I heard Mrs. Danvers say. "She has come home early and if she has gone to the library you can go through the hall and she will not see. I will go and check."

"Hello you little tyke," the man said to Jasper. He came around the morning room and saw me. He was startled at seeing me as if he was master and I the intruder. He was a huge man, eyes indicative of being a heavy drinker, with the smell of whiskey on his breath. His mouth was hot and pink and he gave a smile.

"I didn't expect any visitors this afternoon," I said.

"I just popped in to see old Dann; she is an old friend. How is Old Max?"

It was weird the way he asked after Maxim.

"He is in London," I said.

"And left the bride alone? Isn't he afraid someone will take her away?" He laughed and I did not like it.

Just then Mrs. Danvers came and he said, "Your efforts were in vain Danny, she was hiding here. Won't you introduce us? After all, should one not pay his respects to a new bride?"

Very reluctantly, Mrs. Danvers said, "This is Mr. Favell, Madam."

I asked him, in order to be polite, if he would stay for

tea and I saw that Mrs. Danvers flashed him a warning look not to. He decided that he would rather leave and asked if I wanted to see his car which he had parked further down in order not to disturb me in case I rested in the afternoon.

The lie was very obvious.

"By the way," he said nonchalantly, "it would be nice if you didn't mention my little visit to Max. He doesn't really approve of me and it would get Danny into trouble."

Awkwardly, I said, "No, all right, I won't."

"Bye, then, I will come and look you one day. Shame Max left you alone and went to London."

I walked into the house and rang for my tea.

Nobody came for over five minutes and then a distressed Alice appeared. I asked where Robert was as I wanted my tea under the chestnut tree.

"Robert has gone to the post Madam and Mrs. Danvers gave him to understand that you would be late for tea, Frith is out too, I could bring your tea Madam if you like but it isn't half past four yet," Alice said.

I said I would wait for Robert and assumed that when Maxim was away things slackened.

It was strange that this man had chosen to come when Maxim was not home and it was Frith's day off. It was presumed that I would be late and Robert was sent to the post. Frith and Robert were never away together. Then he asked me not to mention anything to Max. Max — no one called him that except when I had read it once on the fly-leaf of a book in the slanting curious hand. There was something fishy and I didn't want to create a scene, much less, worry Maxim.

As I was waiting in the hall wondering about my tea it occurred to me that this man and Mrs. Danvers were perhaps hand-in-glove about something. They had seen me and shut the window. Were they stealing valuables from the west wing? I decided to go up to the west wing and see it for myself.

The house was quiet, the servants were in their own quarters and I would have enough time before Robert returned.

Presently, I was in the corridor that I had found myself in on the first day, a place I had never been to since and never wanted to. It was very quiet and there was a musty unused smell. The sun streamed in through the window in the alcove. I remembered the room Mrs. Danvers had come out from and went in.

As I switched the light on, I was shocked. The room was fully furnished, there were no dust sheets and it was as if it was in use. There were flowers everywhere, on the dresser, mantelpiece and the table beside the bed. The bed was made and the dresser had brushes powders and scent. There was a dressing gown, bedroom slippers and I thought I was looking back into time.

I went to the window which Favell and Mrs. Danvers had stood at and opened the shutter.

I then began to touch everything — the quilt, the slippers, the monogram on the nightdress case, R de W, I put the nightdress against my face. I walked to the wardrobe and opened it. It was full and there were evening dresses in brocade and velvet and satin.

I heard a step behind me and it was Mrs. Danvers. Her expression was triumphant, gloating, unhealthy and she asked, "Is anything the matter, Madam?" She came closer to me in a sinister way and I thought I would faint. "Are you not well?"

"I'm all right, Mrs. Danvers," I said. "I did not expect to see you and I noticed from the lawns that the shutters were not closed."

"I will close it," she said and walked across the room.

"I had closed it myself but in reality, you wanted to see the room, didn't you? Then why didn't you say so, you had only to ask."

"Now that you are here, I will show it to you, the loveliest room you have ever seen and which you were too shy to ask," she said in an ingratiating tone. I feared and loathed her voice.

"This is her bed," she said, "isn't it beautiful? I keep the golden coverlet because it was her favorite. You have been touching her nightdress, haven't you? Feel it, how soft it is. I haven't washed it since she last wore it. I put out the slippers and her nightdress the day she drowned. I did everything for her, no maid suited her."

"Have you seen her brushes?" she continued. "I have left them unwashed. She used to make me brush her hair, 'hair-drill,' she would say. It was below her waist when she got married and when she cut it everyone was angry but she would say, 'it is nothing to do with anyone.'"

She then began to open the wardrobes. "The sable wrap was a Christmas present from Mr. de Winter. You opened the wardrobe, didn't you, the latch is undone."

"She looked beautiful in this velvet. Put it against your face," she said as she continued the monologue.

As she spoke of Rebecca's death, of what she was wearing that day, of how her body was found battered and without arms she tightened her grip on my arm. She said that Mr. de Winter insisted on going and identifying her and he looked very ill. "I blame myself," she said. "I was in Kerrith and Mrs. de Winter was not expected from London

until later. She had an early dinner and left for the cottage. Had I been there I would not have allowed it. Mr. de Winter was dining with Mr. Crawley at his house."

"The storm was blowing hard and I knocked on Mr. de Winter's room but he said she must be at the cottage. I could not sleep that night and went down to the beach early morning." Mrs. Danvers slowly undid her grip on my arm and her voice became hard again. "One of the life buoys was washed up at Kerrith that afternoon." As she went about straightening the room she said, "Now do you know why Mr. de Winter does not use these rooms? We did up another room for him at the end of corridor but he didn't sleep much there either."

She began to switch the lights off and stood at the door waiting for me to follow. "I dust these rooms myself; no maids are allowed here. Do you suppose the dead come and watch the living. Do you suppose she watches you and Mr. de Winter together?"

She stood looking at me with malicious eyes. "Rober is back now and will bring your tea under the chestnu tree," she said. In a daze, I faltered down the corridor then took the stairs unseeingly. I went to my room, shu the door, put the key in my pocket, went to my bed, an lay down feeling deadly sick.

Chapter 12

Visiting Gran

The next morning, I wondered what I would do with my day. I had slept badly and my damp pillow indicated that I had cried while I slept. At ten o'clock, Frith said that Mrs. Lacy wanted to speak to me.

She said that it was high time I met Gran and we would motor up there in the afternoon. I thought it was a splendid idea as it would break the monotony of the day.

Lunch was a welcome break and punctual at half past three, Beatrice drove up. "You don't look well," she said and as we drove, she asked, "You are not by any chance having a baby, are you? There's nothing to hide if you are, it's nature's way."

She then went on to ask if I was sketching and if I had liked the books she had sent for me.

"Yes, it was a lovely present, Beatrice," I said.

I wondered if I should ask her about Favell and I eventually did. "I think he was Rebecca's cousin," she said. "He probably went to Manderley a lot but I wouldn't know, for I am seldom there."

Rebecca's cousin, I was quite astonished and told her that I hadn't taken much to him and she said she didn't blame me.

We soon approached our destination as we drove past a pair of white gates and a gravel drive. She warned me that the old lady was nearly blind but she had informed the nurse of our visit.

A parlor maid, Norah, opened the door for us and after introductions we were led through a narrow hall and a drawing room with furniture to a veranda facing a lawn.

Maxim's grandmother was sitting there propped up on pillows and surrounded by shawls. I thought she resembled Maxim a lot. The nurse who was reading to her got up and shook hands.

"Dear Bee, how good of you to come, it is dull here," grandmother said.

"This is Maxim's wife," Beatrice said and prodded me to kiss her. She touched my face and said, "You nice thing how good of you to come, you should have brought Maxim too."

"Maxim is in London," I said.

"You may bring him next visit," she said, "and Bee how is Roger? Doesn't come and see me, naughty boy."

"He will come in August. He is leaving Eton and going to Oxford."

"Oh dear, he will be a young man and I shan't know him," grandmother said and Beatrice continued telling her of Giles and Roger.

In some time, the old lady asked complainingly for tea.

"Hungry again after a big lunch?" the nurse asked smiling at her charge.

I felt sorry for the old Gran who must have been young and about Manderley once and now was waiting here to die. Beatrice was glancing at her watch, knowing that she had done her duty for the next three months.

"We have a treat today," the nurse said, "water cress sandwiches."

"Is it water-cress day? Why does Norah not bring the tea?" grandmother said.

"What a time you've been, Norah," the old lady said.

"It's only just turned the half hour, Madam," Norah said and afternoon tea was laid.

We drew our chairs to the table and ate our sandwiches and a smile passed over the old lady's placid face.

Suddenly, grandmother began to ask why Maxim had not come and why she had not brought Rebecca.

"Who is this child?" she asked looking across at me.

"Why did Maxim not bring Rebecca? I am so fond of Rebecca. Where is Rebecca? What have you done to her?

want Rebecca."

The nurse got up and said we had better go for this kind of delirium was likely to last a few hours.

I didn't mind this episode much but poor Beatrice was red faced. In the car, Beatrice said that she was really sorry and had she known this were to happen she would have never brought me.

"There's nothing to be sorry about," I told Beatrice but she continued. "I was a fool to not realize how fond she was of Rebecca. Rebecca used to bring her to Manderley but Gran was more alert then. You see, Rebecca had a knack of being attractive to people, whether men, women, children or dogs. You will never forgive me."

"It's quite alright," I said. Presently we were at the gates of Manderley and bade good bye. I soon approached the house, and saw Maxim's car. My spirits lifted and I ran in. His hat and gloves were on the table. I went to the library and heard loud voices coming in. The door was shut and I hesitated to go in.

"You can tell him to keep away from Manderley," Maxim was saying, "Never mind who told me but I happened to know his car was parked here yesterday afternoon. If you want to meet him you can do so outside Manderley. I will not have him inside the gates and this is the last warning."

I slipped away and hid behind the gallery. Mrs. Danvers came out and shut the door behind her. Her face was angry, horrible and distorted. She went up the stairs quickly to the west wing.

I waited a minute and then slowly went into the library. Maxim's back was turned to me. I thought of creeping out but he turned around and said, "Who is it now?"

"Hello," I said and smiled.

"Oh, it's you…" he said and I could make out that something had made him very angry. "What have you been doing with yourself?"

"Beatrice drove me to see your grandmother," I said.

"How is she? And where is Bee?"

"She had to drive away to meet Giles."

We sat together on the window-seat and I held his hands and told him I had missed him terribly.

"Have you?" he said.

"Was it hot in London?" I asked.

"Yes, I hate the place."

"Are you worried about something?"

"I have had a long day. That drive twice in twenty-four hours is too much," he said.

"I am tired too," I said, "it's been a funny sort of day," and I realized that he was not going to tell me about Mrs. Danvers.

Chapter 13

The Manderley Ball

It was on a Sunday afternoon, Frank Crawley had come up for lunch and we were looking forward to a peaceful afternoon. But that was not to be as we were bombarded by a barrage of unexpected visitors. Tea, which otherwise would have been sandwiches under the chestnut tree, was now a stiff-lipped formal affair in the drawing room with Frith in his element, directing Robert like an orchestra maestro.

I was fumbling with a monstrous silver tea-pot and kettle which I never could manage. Dependable Frank was by my side, helping with the tea cups and the feeble conversation I was trying to make concentrating on the tea-pot. Maxim was playing the perfect host in his own way. It was then that a tedious gushing woman said, "Mr. de Winter, will you be reviving the Manderley Fancy Dress ball?"

"I haven't thought of it," Maxim said, "and no one else here has."

"Oh, but we all have Mr. de Winter," she said.

"But it's a lot of work organizing it and Frank will have to do it all," Maxim said. She turned to Frank Crawley and said, "Oh, please be on my side."

"I don't mind organizing it," Frank said, "it's up to him and Mrs. de Winter," and suddenly all the pleading turned towards me.

"Of course, she longs to have ball in her honor," Lady Crowan persisted. It was settled then and possible dates were discussed. When the visitors, to my relief, at long last bade their adieus, Frank and I went back to enjoy our tea and scones feeling like conspirators.

Frank and I were discussing the ball when Maxim came up to the window with Jasper at his heels. "What will you dress as?" I asked Maxim.

"I never dress up, a perquisite as a host I am allowed," Maxim said.

"What shall I do?" I wondered.

"Put a ribbon round your hair and be Alice-in-Wonderland, you look like it now with the finger in your mouth," he said lightly.

"Don't be rude," I said, "I will surprise you and Frank

with my costume and keep it a secret till I wear it." I headed off with Jasper into the garden and I heard Maxim laugh.

As I walked into the garden with tears stinging me, I speculated whether Rebecca's room was really kept intact because he had ordered it and whether he did go and touch her things as Mrs. Danvers did.

The fancy dress ball was soon a matter of excitement amongst the staff and Clarice was especially excited. She asked me what I would be wearing and I told her I had not decided but whenever I did, it would be a special secret only between the both of us.

I wondered what Mrs. Danvers' reaction to it all was. If she had believed me to be the one to have told Maxim she must hate me even more. I shuddered when I thought of her.

The preparations for the ball were in full swing and I was unable to decide on a costume. I looked through the books Beatrice had given to me in the library, one morning, but everything seemed too elaborate and ostentatious. I made sketches of a few of them but wasn't happy with them and threw them into the waste paper basket.

That evening, as I was changing for dinner, there was a knock on the door and I was startled to see Mrs. Danvers. She had my drawings in her hand and said that the waste paper baskets came to her for checking and Robert had found these and were they important.

I turned cold at the sight of her and said, "No, Mrs. Danvers, it is only a rough sketch."

"Very well, I thought it better to clarify to avoid any misunderstanding," she said and continued to stand by the door.

With a hint of contempt in her voice she asked if I had not been able to decide on what to wear. Then she suggested that I have a look at the pictures in the gallery, especially the one of a young lady in white, with her hat in her hand. I was wondering what had brought on the change in attitude. Did she want to be friends with me or did she know that I wasn't the one to have told Maxim about Favell.

"Hasn't Mr. de Winter suggested a costume for you Madam?" she asked.

I hesitated, then said, "No, I would like it to be a surprise for him and Mr. Crawley."

"Might I suggest, Madam, that you have your dress made in London, and you must study the picture I told you of." As she left the room, she said she would not give my secret away to anyone. The door shut and I wondered what had happened to her?!

I pondered over Favell, Rebecca's cousin? A bounder,

Beatrice had said and he did seem like one. Why did Maxim not want him here? Had Rebecca taken pity on a black sheep in her family?

Over dinner, I was consumed with thoughts of Rebecca and what she must have done, when Maxim interrupted my thoughts and asked, "My little Alice in Wonderland, have you bought your ribbon and sash?"

"I am going to surprise you with my costume, just you wait," I said.

"I am sure you will, now get on with your peaches and don't talk with your mouth full. I am going into the library with my coffee, I have a lot of letters to finish."

I went up to the minstrel's gallery to have a look at the picture especially the one Mrs. Danvers had spoken of. She was Caroline de Winter, a sister of Maxim's great-great grandfather, a woman of great beauty.

The dress would not be difficult to copy, puffed sleeves, the flounce and the bodice, the hat might be difficult and I would need a wig, my straight hair would never lend itself to those curls. The next morning, I sent the sketch to London and got a very favorable response. Now I was as excited as Clarice about the ball.

Only Beatrice and Giles were to spend the night with us, thank heavens, I had heard that in the earlier days people slept on the sofas and in the bathrooms too. I did wonder, if Maxim was having this ball only for my sake.

The preparations lent a buzz to the house, with men coming in to lay the dance floor, the furniture in the drawing room being moved to accommodate buffet tables, lights were being strung everywhere, Frank Crawley came for lunch every day, the servants spoke of nothing else, Frith stalked about as if the whole evening depended on him and Robert had lost his mind. He kept forgetting things and wore a very harassed expression.

Mrs. Danvers was not to be seen but she was orchestrating it all. I, on the other hand, felt quite useless coming in people's way and when once I tried to help by saying where the chairs must go the men gave me a quizzical look, "Those were Mr. Danvers orders," they said. I immediately said, "Yes, of course."

The day dawned misty and cloudy but the mist soon cleared and it was a glorious summer day. The gardeners were bringing flowers by the hundreds into the house and Mrs. Danvers finally appeared, arranging the flowers and directing where the vases should go.

Frank, Maxim and I had lunch at Frank's house so as to be out of the way. I had the same feeling that I had had on my wedding day, too far gone to turn around.

The dress was perfect and the wig was a triumph, thank heaven for that. Maxim and Frank kept digging at me about my costume. Maxim said I should have been Alice in Wonderland whereas Frank believed I would have looked better as Joan of Arc with my straight hair.

"Frank, by this tomorrow all this should be over," Maxim said.

"I hope so, I have given orders that all cars should stand by at 5 a.m.," Frank said seriously.

"I think we better be going up to the house now," Maxim said and I reluctantly followed leaving the comfort of Frank's dining-room.

When we came to the house, the band had arrived and the afternoon dragged like the last hour before a journey. I for one, didn't know what to do with myself. However, soon it was time for tea, after which Beatrice and Giles arrived.

I asked Giles shyly what he would wear and he said that a tailor had made him the dress of an Arabian Sheikh and Beatrice said she was going to match him with some beads and a veil. Naturally then, all eyes turned to me and Maxim said, "She won't tell any of us."

I suddenly felt important and nice that a dance was being given in my honor and I wanted to get started with my clothes. As we went up, I saw how the austere Manderley

had suddenly come alive. There were tables of food, and flowers and the band. The usually cold drawing-room was also a riot of color.

There was a lot of giggling and excitement and rustling of tissue paper when I went to dress and Clarice helped me. I twisted and turned in front of the mirror. "How do I look, Clarice? Give the wig, be careful not to flatten it," I said.

Beatrice was knocking at the door and I told her she couldn't come in and not to let Maxim come in either.

I stared at the face that was looking at me through the mirror barely recognizing myself. I paraded up and down, swishing my flouncy dress. "Oh, Clarice, Oh, Clarice," I said, "open the door and see if all are there." I stood at the head of the stairs and saw Giles in his white Arab dress, Beatrice in green, poor self-conscious Frank, and Maxim in his normal clothes saying, "Where is she? The dinner guests will soon be here."

I stood at the archway and asked the fiddler to stop playing and the drummer to announce me. I whispered to make him beat the drum and say Miss Caroline de Winter. He did that and I stood at the head of the stairs with the hat in my hand, expecting claps and cheers. Beatrice gave a small cry. I smiled and said, "How do you do, Mr. de Winter?"

Maxim stared at me; his face white. Frank went to him but he shook him off. I put one foot on a step and realized something was wrong. Why were they all looking at me like this? Why were they standing there like dummies who were in a trance?

Then Maxim moved forward, he was blazing with anger. "What the hell do you think you are doing?"

"It's the picture in the gallery," I said, terrified. "What have I done? What is it?"

Why were they all staring at me? Maxim spoke and I didn't recognize the cold, icy tone, "Go and change. I don't care what you wear. Wear an ordinary frock, go up before anyone else comes. What are you standing there for? Didn't you hear what I said?"

I turned and ran unseeingly down the archway tripping over my flounces. Tears blinded me and I could not see Clarice. I brushed past the astonished drummer. I looked about like a haunted animal and saw in the west wing the gloating face of a devil as Mrs. Danvers stood there, loathsome, triumphant.

I ran to my room and shut the door. Clarice was waiting for me.

Chapter 14

What an Evening...

Poor Clarice was crying as we both tore my dress apart in a hurry to get it off. I asked Clarice to leave me alone and enjoy the party. Her face was so swollen with tears that I told her to first straighten up and not say anything to anyone. She urged me to find something in my wardrobe which she would iron in a jiffy.

Just then Beatrice came in holding her arms out to me, "My dear, my dear," she said. "Are you all right? Let me get you some water. I knew this was a terrible mistake and you could not have known, how would you?"

"Know what?" I said confused.

"The dress, my dear," Beatrice explained, "the one you copied. It was the same one Rebecca had worn at the last ball. It was identical and when you stood on the staircase..."

"I ought to have known," I said staring, "I ought to have."

"You could not have, my dear, but Maxim, he thinks it was deliberate because you kept it all a secret and you wanted to surprise him. I did tell him that you had not known."

"You can explain it to him later my dear, for now, please come down. The first guests have started arriving and Frank and Giles are going to tell everyone that the store sent the wrong dress to you and no one will be any wiser. Why don't you wear this blue dress, it is so charming."

I refused to go down. "But Maxim will understand," she said and I will try to get him alone and tell him.

"No, no Beatrice please don't. And just tell everyone I have a headache."

"It will look terrible if you don't come, please do, at least for Maxim's sake. Please think of him."

"I think of him all the time, Beatrice," I said.

Just then Giles came up to ask what was happening because the guests had begun to arrive and Maxim had sent him.

"She doesn't want to come, what will we say?" Beatrice said.

"Oh, what a frightful mix-up," Giles said.

"Say that she is feeling faint and will come down a little later. I'll come down and make it all right." Presently, Beatrice straightened her veil and went down.

I looked down from my window at the rose garden and saw the men inspecting the lights as they were coming on. I could picture them all gossiping about where Mrs. de Winter was and how the earlier one was everywhere. Slowly, all the guests would gossip and speak of our marriage being a big failure.

I came back towards my bed, removed the blue dress and looked for a portable iron I used to iron Mrs. Van Hopper's clothes with. I dressed in it, the matching shoes, wiped my earlier make-up off, brushed my hair and went along the corridor.

The hall was quiet and there were voices from the dining room. I walked down the stairs to the open dining room.

When I look back at my first and last party at Manderley, I remember snippets from a vast canvas that was; a very long evening. I stood by Maxim's side to welcome the guests. There were couples dancing, twisting and twirling.

I stood there with a smile on my face and agony in my heart. Maxim stood too with a mask on his face for his guests. Inside he was cold, expressionless, feeling a pain I did not know of.

The evening dragged on. Beatrice whispered in my ear, "Please sit for a while, you look very ill."

"I'm all right."

Giles came and said we should go to the terrace and see the fireworks. There was much excitement and clapping among the crowd.

The band played Auld Lang Syne, and I was relieved to see the guests beginning to leave.

Maxim and Beatrice and I were surrounded by people gushing and thanking for the night. Frank was in the driveway seeing to everyone's cars. Giles was leading some to the buffet tables. Maxim too went out to join Frank.

Beatrice was removing her bangles as she said that the evening was a grand success and I looked lovely in my blue dress and no one had any inkling about the fiasco.

"If I were you, I would lie back in bed tomorrow. Shall I tell Maxim you have gone up?" she asked.

"Yes please, Beatrice."

"All right, sleep well," she said and kissed me swiftly. There were telltale signs of an aftermath of a party, upturned chairs, the band players gone for breakfast. The birds had begun to chirp and the day was breaking as I got ready for bed. My legs were aching and my back had a niggling sensation as I got into bed. My mind refused to rest. The bed beside me looked bare without Maxim and as the day rose, I waited but Maxim did not come.

Chapter 15

The Shipwreck

I had fallen asleep a little after seven. When I woke up, it was broad daylight and the sun was streaming in. Clarice had come and left a tray in which there was cold tea. I saw the bed next to me empty, not having been slept in and the miseries of the previous night came flooding back. I sipped at my tea and wondered if Clarice had noticed and whether it was being discussed amongst the servants.

That was the very reason I had come down last night. I stuck to convention and I didn't want anyone to believe that we had quarreled. Even if Maxim and I lived in two separate corners of Manderley and led separate lives, no one should know of it except the both of us, even the servants must be bribed to stay quiet.

Looking at Maxim's empty bed made me despair that there was nothing worse than a failed marriage that too, of three months. I was not suited to him, we were not companions. I was too young, and moreover, I was not from his world. What was more, I loved Maxim in a hurting and desperate way like a dog or a child.

I could feel Rebecca's presence everywhere and perhaps she could feel mine. I could fight the living but how could I fight the dead?

I noticed a note under my door which Beatrice had written at half past nine when she and Giles had left. Now it was half past eleven. I thought regretfully of how they had been married for twenty years and had a successful marriage unlike my failed marriage of three months.

I dressed and went downstairs. Robert was in the dining room and I asked if he had seen Mr. de Winter. "He went soon after breakfast," he said. I telephoned the office to ask if he was there. Frank came on the line and said that he had not seen Maxim this morning.

"How did he sleep?" he asked.

I did not mind telling Frank, "He did not come to bed last night."

"What did he say last night after everyone had left?"

"I had a sandwich with Giles and Mrs. Lacy, Maxim went into the library," Frank replied.

"Frank, I must see Maxim and explain things. He thinks I did it all on purpose."

"No, no," said Frank.

"It has happened Frank and it has made me realize that Maxim doesn't love me, he loves Rebecca."

Frank said he could not speak on the telephone and it was vital for him to come and see me. I slammed the receiver down. I was crying knowing that I should never see Maxim again.

I went and stared out of the window as a fog was rolling up the sea. I went through the morning room onto the terrace, Jasper standing by my feet. Jasper was with Clarice last night and seemed to have missed me. I looked up at Manderley which was enveloped in a thick mist. The shutter had been pulled aside from the window of the bedroom in the west wing. It was Mrs. Danvers and I knew she was somewhat stalking me. Last night she and Rebecca had triumphed.

I had seen her last night, her devilish smile, and she was a living breathing woman. Not dead like Rebecca. On an impulse I turned around and went into the room to confront her. She was still standing by the window and when I called to her I saw that her eyes were red from crying just as mine were.

"Mrs. Danvers, you have done what you wanted to, haven't you? Are you happy?"

"Why did you ever come here? We were happy without you."

"I love Mr. de Winter."

"If you loved him, you would not marry him." Her voice was thick and choked with tears. "I thought I hated you but now I don't know, all the feelings that I had seem to be spent," she said looking more like a tired, old woman rather than the cruel woman I had seen last night.

"Why do you hate me? What have I done?" I asked.

"You tried to take Mrs. de Winter's place."

"I have not changed a thing at Manderley, I have left everything to you but you set yourself against me from the very beginning. Many men and women marry twice, it is not a crime."

"He is not happy. He's in hell and has been ever since she died."

"That's not true," I said. "We were very happy on our honeymoon."

"Which man would not be?" she said with contempt.

"How dare you say that?" I said as I marched up to her shook her arm and derided her for making Maxim suffer as she did last night, "Would such a vile joke bring Rebecca back to life?"

"Why should I care about his happiness? He hasn't

cared for mine. How does it make me feel to watch you take her place and touch her things? If he suffers let him suffer, he is paying for marrying a young girl in less than ten months while my lady lies cold in the church crypt. She had spirit and was never one to be wronged. I had taken care of her as a child."

"What is the use of all this? Haven't I got any feelings?" I asked but she went on raving like a mad woman. She went on and on and even said how she and Mr. Jack were a pair. Her malicious fingers twisted her black dress. "At sixteen, she drew blood from a horse. She cared for nothing and no one. In the end she was beaten not by a man or woman but by the sea."

She began to sob "I am not ashamed of showing my grief," she continued. "You came here and take my lady's place. Even the servants laugh at you."

"Stop this," I said.

"And then what? You will go running to Mr. de Winter to complain just as you told him of Mr. Jack's visit."

"I did not tell him."

"Then how would he have known? Why should I not see him? He's the only link I have left with Mrs. de Winter. He was always jealous and I wanted to teach you a lesson."

She continued, as if in a spell, "All men were jealous;

she would bring men she met in London to the house over the weekends and take them to the cottage. She lived the way she wanted to. She's Mrs. de Winter, not you, you should go."

I backed away towards the window. "Why don't you go?" she said. "We don't want you, none of us, you ought to be dead. Look down there," she said as I looked below, "it's easy, it's a quick way, not like drowning, just jump. Don't be afraid, I won't push, just jump. Mr. de Winter doesn't love you, you are not happy, jump, jump..." she kept whispering. The fog grew thicker and I could not see anything outside. If I jumped, the pain would be sharp and sudden. Mrs. Danvers kept pushing me to jump. I shut my eyes, there was numbness inside me and I felt giddy. Suddenly, the silence was broken by an explosion that shook the window, there were three or four bursts and I looked at Mrs. Danvers.

"What is it?" I asked stupidly.

"It's the rockets, a ship must have gone ashore along the bay," she said relaxing her grip upon my arm.

We heard the sound of footsteps running below us, on the terrace. It was Maxim, I could not see him but I heard him calling out to Frith. He told Frith the ship was in distress and the house must be kept ready with food and

Mr. Crawley informed. He was going to the cove.

Mrs. Danvers said we must go down as she shut the window, if the sea was running, there would have been no chance for the men. She said that I could tell Mr. de Winter that if he wanted to bring the shipwrecked men up to the house, hot food would be ready for them.

Frith saw me walk down and said, "Did you hear the rockets, madam? Robert and I thought that one of the gardeners had let off a firework from last night. Mr. de Winter was here and has gone back to the beach, a ship has run ashore. He went across the lawn a minute ago."

I began to walk out and saw that the fog was clearing. I looked up at the window at which I was standing five minutes ago. All of a sudden, I began to perspire and feel faint. I went into the hall and called out to Frith for a glass of brandy. Frith came quickly and asked if he should summon Clarice and that perhaps I was exhausted after last night.

I said I would be fine and he then left me alone in the hall which bore no traces of last night. And then like a jolt it struck me that Maxim had not gone away. He was by the cove and seen the ship. His voice was not the voice of yesterday, it was the voice of every day. Maxim was all right

I too went down the steep path to the beach. The fog

was clearing and I could see the ship. I could not see Maxim but Frank was speaking to the coast guards. He waved at me. "Come to see the fun, Mrs. de Winter?" the coast guard asked. He explained that the diver would be sent down to see if the ship had hurt her back.

"Where is Maxim?" I asked Frank.

"He has taken an injured crew to Kerrith to be bandaged. Maxim is splendid, always gives a hand, he will open the house up now for anyone who wants food and a bed," Frank said.

"That is right," said the coast guard. "We need more people like him in the country. He'd give the coat off his back for any of his people."

Soon Frank said he would go back to the office. He asked me to join him for lunch but I preferred to be alone. All the excitement was dying down. The diver would have to make his report.

I was not hungry. I sat on the cliffs, not wanting my lunch. It was past three, I got up and went down the cove. Ben was there. "Seen the steamer?" he asked. "She is Dutch, isn't she?"

"Dutch or German, I don't know," I said.

"She'll break up there," he said, bit-by-bit, he said grinning, "Not sink like stone as the little 'un."

"Who?"

"Her, the other one," he said pointing towards the sea. "The fishes have eaten her up by now."

"Fishes don't eat steamers, Ben," I said. "Good-afternoon Ben, I must go home now."

All the people had gone and I made my way through the woods. The sea was calm. My legs were reluctant and my head was heavy. I seemed to have a strange sense of foreboding in my heart. As I came closer to the house it looked beautiful and peaceful and for the first time with a feeling of pride and joy, I knew that this was my home. Everything here belonged to me.

I went into the dining room and didn't feel like eating the cold meat and salad. I asked Robert if Mr. de Winter had come. He said that he had come in shortly after two, had had a quick lunch and went out again.

"He asked for you and Frith said you must have gone to the ship," Robert said.

"Did he say when he would be back?"

"No, Madam."

I asked Robert to bring my tea into the library and went and sat on the window seat.

I picked up The Times but I was just marking time like a person sitting in a dentist's waiting room. I felt like a new person, the woman in the fancy-dress ball yesterday had been left behind.

Robert brought in my tea and I ate hungrily having just had cold tea at half past eleven.

I was drinking my third cup when Robert came to ask if Mr. de Winter was back.

"Madam, Captain Searle, the harbor-master of Kerrith, is on the telephone. He wants to come and see Mr. de Winter personally."

"I don't know when Mr. de Winter will be back, Robert, please ask him to ring again at five o'clock."

In a few minutes, Robert came back to say that Captain Searle said it was urgent and wanted to see me if that was all right. I said that Robert could ask him to come along at once if he wanted to.

He came soon after the call and I told him that Maxim had been away most of the day. I said that the ship had disorganized everybody. Captain Searle said that the diver had discovered a big hole in its bottom, but that was not why he was here.

"Well, Mrs. de Winter, I don't know how to say this and I don't mean to cause distress to either you or Mr. de Winter as we hold him in high regard, but the past cannot be made to lie quiet. What I am about to say might put you both under the public glare. You see, the diver also discovered the hull of a sailing boat, quite intact. Being a local diver, he recognized the boat to be that of late Mrs. de Winter."

"Do we need to tell Mr. de Winter?" I asked, a fresh blow for Maxim after last night.

"That is not all, you see. The cabin door was closed and he opened it with a stone from the sea bed. There was a body in there, dissolved now," he said in a quieter tone to avoid the servants listening in on us.

"Does that mean she was not sailing alone and someone was with her? But no relative has ever said anything about anyone missing," I whispered quite in shock. "How is it that one body was found here and Mrs. de Winter's was found many miles away?" Now I knew why I had had a sense of foreboding some time ago. There were mysteries that lay beneath the still waters.

"I have to do my duty, Mrs. de Winter, and report the body, keeping aside my personal feelings," he said. Meanwhile, the door opened and in came Maxim asking Captain Searle what the matter was. I couldn't take it anymore and ran out of the room. Maxim looked tired and untidy.

I went to the terrace and believed that in this moment

of crisis I could not be shy and diffident any more. I had to overcome with courage or fail forever. When I heard a car leave, I went into the library where Maxim was standing with his back to the window.

I went and held his hand as he continued to look out. "I am so sorry, Maxim, but I don't want you to bear this alone. I am with you. In twenty-four hours, I have grown up, I am not a child any longer. You have forgiven me, haven't you?"

He gathered me into his arms and said, "What do I have to forgive you for?"

"Last night, you thought I did it on purpose."

"Yes," he said.

"Maxim, please could we start all over again?"

Maxim took my face in his hands and said we had lost all chance at happiness and the thing he most dreaded had happened. Something he thought of day and night. "Rebecca has won," he said. "Her shadow lies between us keeping us from each other. How could I hold you my little love, with fear that this would happen? I remember her eyes and deceitful smile when she died, knowing she would win."

"Maxim," I said softly, "what are you saying? The captain told me about the body, which means she was not alone and you have to find out who it was."

"It is Rebecca's body lying on the floor in the boat. The woman buried in the church was someone unknown. It was not an accident. I killed Rebecca. Shot her in the cottage in the cove. Then I took the boat out, sunk it there, where, today they found it. Now will you still look into my eyes and say that you love me?"

Chapter 16

The Revelation

The silence in the library was palpable. Jasper was licking his foot and the watch on Maxim's wrist was ticking. It made me remember the proverb, 'Time and tide wait for no man.' When people face a calamity, they become numb to any feelings; I felt that way now.

Then something that had never happened before, happened, Maxim took my face in his hands, said, "I love you so much," and kissed me. What I wanted in Monte and Italy was happening now and the surprise of it made me stare emptily.

"But you don't love me anymore, it's too late," he said. "I should have said this four months ago."

"No," I said, coming out of my trance, "No Maxim, please kiss me again, we can't lose each other now. We have to be together — no secrets, no shadows."

"We don't have the time now, maybe a few hours or

days, they have found Rebecca."

"What will happen now?" I said bewilderedly. "What will you do?"

"I don't know, they will identify her body, then they will wonder who the other woman was."

Now I knew why Maxim never spoke of Rebecca, why he looked lost and said, 'something happened a year ago that altered my whole life,' why he had mood swings. It was Maxim who had killed Rebecca.

"Does anyone else know, apart from the both of us?" I asked.

"No, only you and I."

"Frank?" I asked.

"No, there was nobody there except me," he said.

He sat on a chair and I knelt beside him. I told him that I loved him very much. He spoke of how he went mad after that, living a life of lie, answering letters of sympathy, facing the staff, not being able to let Mrs. Danvers go, for with her knowledge of Rebecca she might have guessed. Poor Bee and Giles asking why he looked frightfully ill.

"I almost told you once, when Jasper ran to the cove," he said.

"Why didn't you? We have wasted all this time that we could have been together?"

"I thought you were unhappy and bored and I am so much older than you. You seemed so shy and always had more to say to Frank."

"How could I get close to you knowing all the while that it was Rebecca you loved and she who was on your mind? I thought whatever you did with me, in your mind you said, 'I did this with Rebecca.' Was that true?" I asked.

"Oh my God," he said and he pushed me away and began walking up and down the room. I watched him puzzled as I sat crouched on the floor.

"I didn't kill her because I loved her, I killed her because I hated her. She was incapable of love. A vicious woman, with no decency. She wasn't even normal. Our marriage was a mockery from the very beginning.

Rebecca was very clever. She had a way with people. Had you met her she would have walked with you in the woods and spoken of painting or whatever was your interest. When I married her, everyone said how lucky I was. Even Gran, who is so difficult to please, said that she had the three things that mattered in a wife, 'beauty, brains and breeding.' I discovered her revolting and deceiving nature five days after we were married. You remember the drive to that hill in Monte Carlo? She had sat there laughing, her hair blowing in the wind, telling me things I cannot repeat to a soul and I knew then what creature I had married."

The jigsaw puzzle started falling into place, Maxim went to the window and began to laugh. He laughed like a man haunted. I was frightened. "Maxim!" I cried.

"That day I was tempted to push her," he continued. "It would have been easy. I terrified you too, that day, remember? Living with the devil, strips you of all sanity. She made a bargain with me that day and said, "I will look after your Manderley and make it the most famous place in the country. People will envy us and talk of us being the luckiest and handsomest couple in the world." She sat there laughing and tearing at a flower.

I came back to Manderley and began a life of lie. I could not bear to stand in a divorce court and reveal to the world everything that she had revealed to me. It would be too shameful, all the country speaking of us. She knew I would sacrifice everything for my pride. I thought of Manderley too much, and this kind of love can never thrive. You hate me now, don't you?" he asked looking at me. "Can you understand my shame and disgust? Do you despise me?"

I didn't care about his shame or any of the things he had said. What mattered to me was that Maxim didn't love Rebecca and that made my heart sing.

"I cannot even tell you about those shameful and filthy days. We would pretend in front of friends, family and the poor servants. She would laugh at them behind their back. The place would be full here for a party or pageant, she would put her arm through mine and give away prizes to little children. Then at the crack dawn she would go to her flat in London for unspeakable things. She made Manderley look the way it does now — the azaleas, the garden, the Happy Valley. My father knew nothing about the garden or furniture or pictures, some things were just stored away. I kept my side of the bargain and didn't give her away."

I let him talk, that his bitterness and pent-up hatred might come loose. He continued, "At first, she was careful, then slowly, she started bringing people to the house, she had picnics in the cottage by the cove. I once found her there with half a dozen people. Then she started hitting on poor faithful Frank. I only caught it when one day Frank said he wanted to resign and began to cry. When I confronted her, she used foul language and went away for a month. Bee had guessed her nature and didn't quite like her. Slowly, things began to fall into place and I wished I had known of all this earlier."

"She had a cousin, Jack Favell, who began to come here."

"I know, he was here when you were in London."

"Why didn't you tell me? I heard it from Frank who saw him at the lodge gates."

"I thought that if I told you of him, it would remind you of Rebecca," I said.

"As if I need reminding. Favell had a black, filthy record. She would spend the night with him in the cottage and I could not stand him being in Manderley and I warned her. One day, she went to London and came back the same day which was unusual. I dined with Frank and when I came, I saw her things but she was nowhere in the house. I went to look for her at the cottage. I took my gun to scare Favell but she was alone. I told her I had had enough of this sham, 'this is your last chance.'

'You are right, Max, I should turn a new leaf,' she said mocking me. She said that I would never be able to prove a thing against her in the court of law. She laughed at what Frank and Beatrice would be able to say. 'I have the backing of Danny and all the servants; we could make you look so foolish.'

She taunted me that even if she had a child no one in the world would know that it is not mine. It would grow up in Manderley as an heir for my precious Manderley and she would play the part of a loving mother just as she did of a loving wife. 'Now, I will turn a new leaf, won't I?' she said laughing madly, 'And all the smug locals and blasted tenants will be so happy and nobody will ever guess. You would be thrilled, Max, wouldn't you want to watch my son grow bigger? How supremely funny, Max,' and she turned to me smiling. When I killed her, the bullet went straight through the heart and she was still smiling and still standing. Even her eyes were open…" he said trailing off.

His hand was cold in mine and he said that he didn't realize that there would be so much blood.

"I went back and forth to the cove to carry water. Even the window went back and forth as I sat there with a bucket and a washcloth. I carried her to the boat; it was half past eleven, nearly twelve. I had never sailed with Rebecca and I struggled a bit with the boat. It was very dark. I was struggling in the wind. I managed to go down to the cabin. We were getting near the ridge, I had to work fast. I opened the sea cocks and split the planks. I climbed into a dinghy and saw the boat drifting away and sinking. I went back to the shore. It had begun to rain. I wondered if someone could hear it all. I went to the house and into my dressing room. Mrs. Danvers came to say she was worried about Rebecca, I asked her to go back to sleep. I went to the window and watched the rain. That is my story. I should have taken her out in the bay, there, they would never have found her; she was too close in."

"It was the ship," I said.

"I knew it would happen. Even when I went to Edgecoombe. Rebecca would win, I can't forget the smile when she died. She has won and loving you has made no difference."

"Rebecca is dead," I said, "She cannot bear witness. We have to think of a way out. It could be the body of someone you don't know. A body does rot in water, doesn't it?"

"Her things will be there, her rings or something, the body was not battered at sea, just lying in the sea," he said.

I asked what would happen now and he said that Captain Searle had made arrangements for five thirty the next morning when no one would be about to try and raise the boat. "He is sending his boat to pick me up in the cove. He will try to raise the boast and drain out the water. There will be a doctor."

"If they say the body is Rebecca's, you must say that the one at Edgecoombe was a ghastly mistake and you were very ill. Nobody saw you that night, only you and I know of it," I said.

Just then the telephone rang in the little room in the library and Max shut the door and went to answer it. My

heart felt free for I knew that Maxim did not love Rebecca. Now that I knew what a rotten woman she was, I didn't hate her and I wasn't afraid of her. She could not hurt me or haunt me every time that I went into a room or touched a thing.

I had grown up; I wasn't a shy child anymore and I would not allow Rebecca to win.

Maxim said it was Colonel Julyan and as the magistrate of Kerrith he would be present too tomorrow and Inspector Welch.

"Why them?" I asked.

"It is the custom when a body is found," he said.

"Colonel Julyan asked if it was possible that I had made a mistake at Edgecoombe?"

"Already? And what did you say?"

"That it might have been possible."

"They may not be able to raise the boat," I said. "Then they couldn't do anything about the body, could they?"

"I don't know," he said and the telephone rang again.

Maxim returned and with a pain in the pit of my stomach I asked who it was.

"It has started," Maxim said. "The reporters asking if it was Mrs. de Winter's boat and was there a body? Now it will soon be everywhere."

"What did you say?"

“That I did not know and did not have a statement to make.

“Oh, but you may want them at your side.”

“I would rather fight alone without a newspaper behind me,” he said.

The next morning, I woke up at seven and I knew that Maxim must have left at five. I went down for breakfast as usual at nine and Frith asked if he should keep the breakfast hot for Maxim. I said that he had to go out early.

I went into the morning room and noticed that the windows had not been opened and the room had not been cleaned. I rang for the under-housemaid and told her the room had not been touched this morning and I did not want that happening again. Even the dead flowers were not cleared. I had not known that being firm was so easy. The menu for the day lay on the table and I realized the cold food on it was what was left over from the ball. I called Robert and asked him to tell Mrs. Danvers to give us something hot. Then I went to the rose garden and cut some buds to arrange in the vases.

Just as I was finishing, Mrs. Danvers came in to ask why I had sent the message with Robert. I told her that if the kitchen did not like the cold food it could be thrown. “Anyway, so much is wasted, a little more wouldn’t matter.”

She continued to stare at me and said she was not used to orders being sent through Robert. "If Mrs. de Winter wanted anything changed, she'd ring me personally."

"I'm afraid that doesn't concern me, for I am Mrs. de Winter now and if I want to send a message with Robert, I shall," I said.

Robert came in to say that the County Chronicle wished to speak with me and I asked Robert to say I was not home. Mrs. Danvers continued to wait and I told her she could leave as I was busy. She wanted to know why the County Chronicle wished to speak with me.

"Is it true?" she asked me. "That Mrs. de Winter's boat has been found, Frith brought the story back with him from Kerrith last night. Captain Searle was here last night. Why was Mr. de Winter up so early? Is it true that a body was found? Mrs. de Winter always sailed alone."

"It is no use asking me anything, Mrs. Danvers, I only know as much as you do," I said. She can't frighten me anymore I thought.

I was walking up and down on the terrace at half past eleven and Frith came to say that Mr. de Winter was on the telephone. He was at the office and called to say that Frank and Colonel Julyan would join us for lunch at one o'clock. I waited for him to say more but he only said that they had managed to raise the boat and he was just back from the creek.

At one o'clock they came in and Maxim and Frank went for a wash while Colonel Julyan stood by the window with me. "This is so distressing for you and your husband Mrs. de Winter and I do feel for you. What makes it difficult was the first body your husband identified." He slowly said then that the evidence this morning pointed to the body being hers although he could not go into details then. "The evidence was sufficient for your husband and Doctor Phillips to identify."

Just then Maxim said lunch was ready and the conversation around the lunch table veered towards the weather. We knew that Frith was behind us and pretenses had to be kept.

"I was saying to your wife, Mr. de Winter, the awkward situation of you having identified the earlier body," Colonel Julyan said.

"The mistake was natural," Frank immediately said, "he was very ill when the authorities asked him to come."

"Now all that is in the past. I do wish you could be spared the publicity and formality of an inquest, but it must be done. It should not take long. Just reconfirm the identification and get Tabb, who you said converted the boat when your wife brought her from France, to say that it was sea-worthy," Colonel Julyan said.

"That's all right, we understand," Maxim said.

Frank was looking at Maxim. Frank knew and Maxim did not know that he knew. "Accidents happen even to the most experienced people," he said.

"Well, we will never know. I shall arrange for the inquest on Tuesday and make it as short as possible. However, I am afraid we won't be able to keep the reporters out. Thank you for a splendid lunch, hope you won't mind my dashing away, I have quite an afternoon ahead of me. Crawley, would you like a ride till your office?"

When they had gone, Maxim took my arm and we stood on the terrace.

"It's going to be all right," he said. "There was never a question; Doctor Phillips could have identified her even without me, but there was no trace of what I had done, for the bullet had not touched the bone. They all say that she was trapped there and the jury will believe it too."

I was quiet and he continued, "I don't regret what I have done, I would do it again, I only mind for you. When I looked at you at lunch, I saw that the funny young look you had on you that I loved, has gone ever since I told you about Rebecca. You are now much older…"

Chapter 17

The Inquest

That evening, when Frith brought in the paper, the headlines were splashed all across. Maxim had gone up to change. Frith kept waiting there and I thought it would be foolish to ignore something that mattered so much to all of them.

"It's all so dreadful, Frith," I said. "So painful for Mr. de Winter."

"Yes, Madam; we are all very distressed outside. I wonder how Mrs. de Winter could have trapped herself, she was very experienced."

"Accidents do happen Frith and how it all happened we will never know," I said.

"It is very difficult to keep the matter from being discussed outside although I am trying," Frith said. "Especially the girls, Robert I can handle. The news has been a great shock to Mrs. Danvers. She has been in her room since lunch and Alice said she looked very ill indeed."

"Yes, Frith, I imagined it would be. And if she is ill, no use she seeing to things. I can manage the ordering."

Frith then left and I glanced at the paper before Maxim came down.

When Frank came up after breakfast, the next day, he looked tired and pale. "I have asked the exchange to put all calls to Manderley through the office whoever it might be," he said.

"If it is reporters, I will handle them. Mrs. Lacy called to say she would like to come to the inquest."

"Oh my God..." Maxim said.

"I prevented that and said that it would be of no use and Mr. de Winter wished to see no one except Mrs. de Winter. She asked me when it was and I said the date has not been decided. However, if she reads it in the papers, we cannot stop her from coming."

"Those blasted reporters," Maxim said.

"You focus on your statement at the inquest. Please remember that Old Horridge is the Coroner, he's a sticky fellow and goes into irrelevant details just to impress the jury. You must not get rattled."

"Why should I be rattled?" Maxim said.

"These coroners' inquests can make one quite nervy

and irritable and the last thing you want is to get his back up."

"Frank is right," I quickly said. "The faster this is over, the faster we can all put this behind us and move on."

Now there was nothing to do but to wait for Tuesday. The inquest would be at two o'clock.

On Tuesday, we had lunch at quarter to one. It was a hurried and anxious meal. Frank came. Thank goodness that Beatrice telephoned to say that she could not come because Roger had the measles and they were all quarantined.

Frank followed us in his car. As we drove, Maxim and I sat quiet. The inquest was to be at Lanyon, a market town, six miles the other side of Kerrith. We parked our car in the cobbled square by the market-place. Doctor Phillips' car and Colonel Julyans' cars were already there as were many others.

I decided that I would wait in the car and Maxim was happy for he had wanted me to wait at Manderley itself. I walked about the streets which were not busy and somehow found myself at the building where the inquest was taking place. I wondered what was happening inside.

A policeman recognized me and asked if I wanted to wait inside and showed me to a bare room. I was getting very restless and walked to the passage. The policeman was there and I asked him how long he supposed it would take. He offered to go in and check and said that it would not be much longer as Mr. de Winter, Captain Searle, the diver and Doctor Phillips had given their evidence and only Mr. Tabb, the boat-builder, was required to give his.

Then he said, "Would you like to hear it? There is a seat inside the door and if you slip in no one will notice you."

I decided to go in because Maxim had given his evidence. It was him I didn't want to hear. The rest didn't matter.

I went into the room and kept my head low because I did not want anybody to see me. The room was very small, hot and stuffy. From the corner of my eye, I saw Mrs. Danvers and Jack Favell and my heart gave a jump.

Mr. Tabb began his evidence. "I converted Mrs. de Winter's boat into a yacht."

"Was the boat in a fit state to be put to sea?" the coroner asked.

"It was when I fitted her out in April last year. It was Mrs. de Winter's fourth season since the conversion."

"Had the boat ever been known to capsize?"

"No sir, Mrs. de Winter was delighted with it in every way."

“And great care is needed to handle the boat?”

“Sir, everyone has to have their wits about them when they go sailing but Mrs. de Winter’s boat was a sturdy one and she had sailed it in worse weather than what was there that night.”

The coroner continued to question, “But, if she went below for a coat and there was a sudden puff of wind, would the boat capsize?”

“No, it wouldn’t,” said Tabb adamantly.

“Well,” said the coroner, “neither does Mr. de Winter nor do I suspect your workmanship. Unfortunately, accidents happen and, in that minute, when Mrs. de Winter relaxed her watchfulness, the boat went down.”

“Excuse me, sir, there is something more I want say. Last year, after the incident, a lot of things were said about my work. They said that I had given Mrs. de Winter a leaky, rotten boat and I lost two or three orders because of it. Yesterday, when the boat was brought up, I requested Captain Searle to allow me to inspect it. When I did, I saw that there was absolutely nothing wrong with the boat. She was lying on sand and no rock had touched her.” The coroner gave him an expectant look. He continued, “What I would like to know is who drove the holes in her planking? They were done with a spike.”

I felt as if there was a deathly silence and I continued to stare at the floor.

"What sort of holes?" asked the coroner.

"There were three of them, sir, and the sea-cocks that plug the pipes from the wash basin and lavatory were also open sir. If the sea-cocks are open, water flows in. Yesterday, I saw that the sea-cocks were completely turned on; with those open and the holes in the plank, a small boat like hers would take not more than ten minutes to sink. Those holes were not there when the boat left my yard. Sir, it is my opinion that the boat did not capsize, it was scuttled."

The room felt very hot. Why were there no windows? I must try and get out. I could hear everyone talking. I could hear 'Mr. de Winter'; I knew the feeling; when I was with Mrs. Danvers at the window, Mrs. Danvers was here too. The heat was slowly rising upon me and touching every bit of me.

The coroner was saying, "Mr. de Winter, do you know anything of these holes? Is it the first time you are hearing of them? Is it a shock to you?"

"It was shocking enough for me to learn that I had identified the wrong body and now to know that the boat was deliberately sunk! Should I not be shocked?"

'Oh, no, Maxim,' I thought. 'Not in this tone, please don't be angry, don't get his back up.'

"Mr. de Winter, please do believe that we all feel very deeply for you and that is why I am inquiring into the matter. This inquiry is not for my own amusement."

"That's rather obvious, isn't it?"

"I hope it is. Do you doubt the statement made by James Tabb here?"

"Of course not, he is a boat-builder and knows what he is talking about?"

"Who looked after Mrs. de Winter's boat?"

"She looked after it herself."

"The boat was moored in the private harbor belonging to Manderley. Any stranger who tampered with the boat would be seen? There is no access by public footpath?"

"No, none."

"The harbor is quiet and surrounded by trees. It is a possibility that a trespasser might not be noticed."

"Yes."

"James Tabb says that a boat with holes and sea cocks open could not have stayed afloat for more than ten minutes. Had that been the case the boat would have sunk at her moorings."

"Undoubtedly."

Therefore, we assume that whoever took the boat out to sea that night drove the holes and opened the sea-cocks.

"The statement of Doctor Phillips and Captain Searle and you says that the cabin door was shut, the port-holes closed and your wife's remains were on the floor."

"Yes," Maxim said.

"Does it not seem strange that now we hear that spikes were driven through the bottom and the sea-cocks were opened?"

"Absolutely."

"Do you have any suggestions to make?"

"No, none at all."

"Mr. de Winter, painful as it might be, I need to ask, were relations between you and the late Mrs. de Winter perfectly happy?"

They did come, the black spots dancing in front of my eyes, the air was so hot, the floor seemed to be coming up to meet me and through the mist I could hear Maxim's voice saying, "Will someone take my wife outside? She is going to faint."

When I came to, I was sitting in the waiting room again. The policeman was hovering over me and Frank was holding me. "I am so sorry," I said, "such a stupid thing to do. It was so very hot in there."

"It does get very airless in there. There have been many complaints but no one does anything," the policeman said.

Frank said that Maxim had asked him to take me back to Manderley. I wanted Frank to stay with Maxim and I wanted to stay too. But Frank insisted.

"They will have to go over the evidence again," Frank said in the car. "The coroner might ask questions in a different way. Tabb's evidence has changed everything."

"The coroner, I am afraid Frank, will make Maxim lose his temper and make him say things he doesn't mean."

Frank was quiet and I knew he was worried. He dropped me at the steps.

I lay down on my bed and must have fallen asleep, because when I woke up with a start it was five and I ran onto the terrace where there was thunder and lightning and a drop or two of rain. I asked Robert if the men were back and he said no. At long last, about half past five, Maxim drove up in his car. My legs felt like straw, Maxim looked so old and tired.

"It's over," he said. "Suicide. There was not sufficient evidence. They all seemed at sea."

"Suicide," I whispered as I sat on the sofa. "And what was the motive?"

"They didn't seem to believe a motive was required. Old Horridge asked if she had money troubles? Money troubles?! God heavens!"

"Why were you so long but?" I asked.

"He went over and over the same things again and again. I kept my temper though, seeing you by the door made me remember what I had to do. I am so tired darling. I can't see or feel anything."

Maxim sat on the window-seat and I sat beside him. Frith and Robert performed the ritual of tea and I asked where Frank was.

"Gone to the vicar," he said. "I would have gone too but I wanted to come back to you."

"Why the vicar?" I asked.

It then occurred to me that Rebecca would have to be brought back from the mortuary and buried.

"I wish you didn't have to go out again," I said.

"We'll talk things over this evening when I get back. We'll begin all over again. I have been the worst sort of husband for you."

"Let me come with you, please. I shan't mind."

"No, I don't want you to come."

He left the room and I heard the car starting. Robert came to clear the tea away. My mind wandered to the crypt of the church.

Ashes to ashes. Dust to dust. It seemed to me that Rebecca had no reality any more.

Chapter 18

The Blackmail

At seven, the rain began to fall, gently at first and then a faster torrent. Frith came in to ask if Mr. de Winter would be long. There was a gentleman insistent on seeing him.

"Who is it Frith?"

"It's a gentleman who used to come here often when Mrs. de Winter was alive. His name is Mr. Favell."

I shut the window as the rain was coming in, and stood by the fireplace. "I will see him, Frith," I said hoping that I would be able to get rid of him before Maxim arrived. I was not afraid of him. When he walked in, his eyes were bloodshot, perhaps he drank a lot.

"Maxim is not here," I said "and I don't know when he will be back. It is best you make an appointment at the office tomorrow."

"Waiting doesn't worry me. He hasn't run off, has he? Under the circumstances, a wise thing to do. Gossip is unpleasant and best avoided, isn't it?"

He didn't tell me why he wanted to see Maxim and instead, made himself comfortable on the sofa. I said, "Mr. Favell, if you don't mind, please will you see Maxim at the estate office tomorrow, I have had a long and exhausting day."

"It has been exhausting for me too," he said, as he came towards me. "This business has been a shock to me too, Rebecca was my cousin and I was very fond of her."

"I am sorry for you," I said.

"We were brought up together. We liked the same things, the same people, the same jokes. She was very fond of me and I was fonder of Rebecca than anyone else."

"Yes," I said.

"And I am going to see justice is done. That old fool coroner got taken in, but you and I both know it isn't suicide, don't we?"

Just then, the door opened and Maxim and Frank came in. "What the hell are you doing here?" Maxim said.

"Congratulations on the inquest, Max," he said.

"Will you leave the house or should we have you thrown out?"

"Shut the door if you don't want Frith to hear what I have to say." Frank quietly closed the door.

"Now listen, Max, it was touch and go but you have come out of this fairly well, I must say. Did you square the jury?"

Maxim made a move towards Favell, but he held up his hand.

"Max, I can make things not only unpleasant for you but also dangerous."

"I suppose there are no secrets between you two and Frank here makes a happy trio," he said. "Everyone knows Rebecca and I were lovers. I was shocked to hear of her death but then I thought that was Rebecca, she would go out the way she lived, fighting. Then I heard of the incident and wondered who could have been with Rebecca? I believed the story until Tabb gave his evidence. What about those holes and sea-cocks? Suicide, eh?"

"You heard the evidence and you heard the verdict. After all these hours, I am not going into with you again. It satisfied the coroner, let it satisfy you."

"I have a note here that might interest you. It was the last thing she wrote, let me read it for you—

I tried to ring you from the flat but got no answer. I'm going down to Manders right away. I shall be at the cottage this evening, and if you get this in time, will you get the car and follow me. I'll spend the night at the cottage and leave the door open for you. I've got something to tell you and I want to see you as soon as possible.

Rebecca.

Is this what you write before you commit suicide? I found this note at four in the morning and didn't fancy a six-hour drive. When I put a call through to her at twelve, I heard that she had been drowned. Had I given this note to the coroner, things would have been tricky for you."

"Well, then why didn't you?" Maxim asked.

"Steady Max, steady, you have never been a friend to me and all men with lovely wives are jealous. I see no harm in sharing women, though. Now, let me lay my cards on the table. I am not a rich man and I am very fond of gambling. If we settle at two to three thousand a year, for life, I swear before God, I will never trouble you again."

"What is the amount you are looking at?" Frank asked.

"Don't interfere, Frank, this is my affair entirely and I won't concede to blackmail."

Favell laughed and said, "I don't suppose your wife wants to be called the widow of a murderer who was hanged."

"I am not afraid of anything, Favell, you cannot frighten me, there is a telephone there, should I call Colonel Julyan, the magistrate, and he shall be interested in your story."

Favell laughed, "Good bluff, Max, you wouldn't dare do it. I have enough evidence against you."

Maxim walked quietly into the other room and I beseeched Frank to stop him. Frank went towards the door but Maxim said, "Leave me alone."

He put a call through to Colonel Julyan and asked if he could come right away to Manderley as there was an urgent matter. He came back to say that Colonel Julyan would be here presently.

"Maxim," Frank tried to say.

Favell laughed, picked a paper and flung himself on the sofa, "If you want to hang yourself, old fellow, it's all the same to me."

Frith soon showed Colonel Julyan in.

"I have brought you out Colonel, in this weather, for a purpose. This is Jack Favell, my late wife's first cousin, whom you might have met. Go ahead, Favell."

Favell did not seem very pleased at the turn of events. "You see, Colonel," he said in a loud voice, "I am not satisfied with the verdict today."

"Isn't that for Mr. de Winter to say?"

"No, not only was Rebecca my cousin, but my prospective wife had she lived."

Taken quite aback, Colonel Julyan asked, "Is that right

Mr. de Winter?"

"It's the first I have heard of it," Maxim said.

"What exactly are you getting at?" Colonel Juyan asked.

Favell produced the note from his pocket and asked the Colonel if someone who wanted to commit suicide would have written it.

Favell said that Rebecca going for a sail didn't surprise him, it was what she would do after a long day in London, but she had made an appointment with him, "But deliberately drown herself, oh no!" Favell was shouting and that did not go down well with Colonel Julyan.

"My dear fellow, there is no use losing your temper with me, I was neither the coroner this morning nor the jury. We all heard the evidence. What exactly are you getting at?"

Favell turned his head towards Maxim, "Rebecca did not commit suicide, she was murdered. And the murderer stands before you with a smug smile on his face, Maximilian de Winter. He couldn't even wait a year to marry the first girl he set eyes upon. He would look good hanging, wouldn't he?"

Favell then began to laugh loud like a drunkard all the while twisting Rebecca's note in his hands. Thank God for his flushed face and bloodshot eyes. It made Colonel Julyan hostile and put him on our side.

"This fellow is drunk," he said.

"Drunk, am I? There are other magistrates in the country, who understand justice, not a retired incompetent soldier like you."

"If you felt so deeply at the inquest today, why didn't you say anything?"

"I wanted to tackle de Winter personally."

"That is why I called you, Colonel, I asked him the same question. He said that he was not a rich man and if I could settle two or three thousand on him for life, he would never trouble me. My wife and Frank here are witness."

"That is true, sir," said Frank.

"You see blackmail is never simple and can land even innocent people in jail. Have you any proof Mr. Favell to back your accusations? Is there a witness?"

"Witness be damned. He knew I was her lover; he was jealous, she was waiting for me at the cottage. He went down that night, killed her and sank the boat."

"Get me a witness," Colonel Julyan repeated.

"Hang on, I could produce a witness, there's a good chance he could have seen," Favell said.

While the others wondered, I instinctively knew who it would be.

"There's a half-wit who spends his time on the beach. I have often seen him and he used to see me come. There's a good chance he could have seen."

"Can we get him here for questioning?" Colonel Julyan asked.

"Of course," Maxim said, "Frank please ask Robert to go and fetch him from his mother's cottage."

"You have a little trade union running here, haven't you? The magistrate won't say anything, a wife doesn't speak against her husband, thus the bride is exempted, Crawley here would lose his job. And Crawley has a bit of malice against me, doesn't he? He was not very successful with Rebecca, were you? This time the bride will be very grateful for your fraternal arm whenever she faints, and the arm will be especially handy when the judge sentences her husband to death."

Maxim's blow came so hard and fast that before anyone knew what was happening, Favell was on the floor. He staggered back on his feet and demanded a drink. Frank brought him a whiskey. Colonel Julyan came to me and said I had better go up but I wanted to stay.

Frank went out into the hall to bring Ben in when he heard the car. "All right Ben, there's nothing to be afraid of; Mr. de Winter wants to give some cigarettes to you."

Ben looked dazed and dreadful, he kept blinking his eyes because of the lights and twisting his sou'wester. I gave him a tremulous smile but I don't know if he recognized me. Favell asked Ben if he knew who he was. Ben didn't say anything. Then Colonel Julyan explained gently that he would soon go home; they only wanted him to answer a few questions.

"Have you seen him?" Colonel Julyan asked.

"I never seen 'un," he said.

"Don't be a fool, you have seen me go into Mrs. de Winter's cottage, haven't you?

"No," said Ben, "I never seen no one."

"You half-witted liar! Haven't you seen us go into the cottage? You were even peering through the window once."

"Eh?" Ben said.

"A convincing witness," Colonel Julyan said sarcastically.

"Someone has bribed this idiot; he has seen me many a times. Here, will this make you remember?" he asked removing his note case

"I never seen 'un. Has he come here to take me to the asylum?"

"No, Ben, of course not," said Frank.

"You remember Mrs. de Winter?" Colonel Julyan asked and Ben glanced at me. "No, not this one, the other lady

who used to go to the cottage."

"She's gone," he said.

"Were you there on the beach twelve months ago when she went sailing and didn't come back?"

"Eh?"

"You saw Mrs. de Winter go into the cottage and Mr. de Winter, too, didn't you?" Favell persisted.

Ben went against the wall, "I seen nothing. I want to stay home. I'm not going to the asylum. I never seen you never before. I never seen you and she in the woods."

"You crazy little rat," Favell said.

"This performance has been a waste of time," Colonel Julyan said. "Is there anything more you want to ask?"

"It's a plot," shouted Favell. "Someone has paid him."

He turned to Favell, "You have not produced a suitable witness."

Favell rung the bell and I knew what he would do. He asked Frith to get Mrs. Danvers. Frith looked at Maxim and Maxim nodded his head. Favell explained to the Colonel that Mrs. Danvers was Rebecca's personal friend and had almost brought her up.

"You are going to find Danny a very different sort of witness, unlike Ben who was given a pat on his back and supper for being a good boy. This time it won't be very easy

for the trade union."

Mrs. Danvers came in. She seemed shrunk and wizened. Colonel Julyan asked Mrs. Danvers if she was aware of the relationship between Mrs. de Winter and Mr. Favell? She replied that they were cousins.

"Oh, come on Danny, weren't we in love?" Favell said.

"She was not," Mrs. Danvers said.

"You old fool…"

"She was not in love with anybody, not you, not Mr. de Winter. She hated all men. She was above it all."

"Didn't she come down to the cottage to meet me and to London?" Favell said flushed with anger.

"And what if she did?" Mrs. Danvers said. "She had a right to amuse herself. She laughed at you all, she would come up and sit on the bed and rock with laughter."

There was silence in the room as her revolting words left everyone in disbelief. Colonel Julyan asked if she thought there was any reason why Mrs. de Winter should have wanted to commit suicide?

"No," she said.

"See, I told you," Favell said.

"Be quiet, will you?" Colonel Julyan said. "Please show the note to her."

Mrs. Danvers read the note twice and said that if there

was anything important to say, Mrs. de Winter would have told her first.

"Did you see her that night?"

"No, I was spending the afternoon and evening at Kerrith and will never forgive myself for that."

Colonel Julyan asked anyone know how she spent her day in London?

"Mrs. de Winter had a hair appointment from twelve until one thirty. I had booked it for her. Then she always lunched at the club so she could leave the pins in there."

"What was she doing until three, we must ascertain that, if Favell says the porter saw her at his flat at three," Colonel Julyan said.

"I have her diary," said Mrs. Danvers, "where she methodically wrote her appointments and then crossed them off. If it will be helpful, I will go and fetch it."

"Do you mind de Winter if we see it?"

"Of course not," said Maxim.

I went and stood at the window, the fury of the rain had been spent and it wasn't falling quite so hard.

Mrs. Danvers came with the diary and Colonel Julyan removed his spectacles to look at the red book — the hair appointment and lunch at the club were there, with crosses against them. "What do we have here?" he said. "Baker, two o'clock. Who was Baker?"

Maxim shook his head and Mrs. Danvers said that she had never heard of the name before.

"There's a cross against the name. If we could find who Baker was, we could get to the bottom of this. Was she in the hands of money-lenders?"

Mrs. Danvers gave him a scornful look. "Mrs. de Winter?"

"Was anyone threatening her or blackmailing her?"

"She was afraid of nothing and no one. She was only scared of old age, of sickness and lying in bed. She wanted to go quickly like a candle snuffed and that was my only consolation. Drowning is painless, isn't it?" Mrs. Danvers said.

Favell was getting impatient. Just then Mrs. Danvers found a number against Baker in the diary. It was 0488 but no exchange. Colonel Julyan took a closer look and said there was an M.

"Mayfair 0488! What a genius; and Danny what a sleuth you are getting to be in your old age."

Maxim asked Frank to put the call through. He was waiting for the exchange to put him through while Colonel Julyan was walking up and down, his hands behind his back. Then the telephone rang in its shrill tone and Frank came back to say that a Lady Eastleigh lives at Mayfair 0488 and they have never heard of Baker.

Favell laughed, "The butcher, the baker, the candle-stick maker, they all jumped out of a rotten potato, carry on Detective Number One, what is the next exchange on the list?"

"Try Museum," Mrs. Danvers said. And the same sham was repeated.

I knew who Baker was and I had known all along, I wished he would not be found. Poor Frank who loved Maxim did not realize that that piece of evidence was a dagger that could kill Maxim. "It was a night porter from an address in Bloomsbury. There are no residents; the place is used as a doctor's consulting rooms. Baker's given up practice and left six months ago, but the porter gave me his address."

When Maxim looked at me it was as if he was bidding farewell and for a moment it was only the two of us in the room suspended in time.

Chapter 19

Unravelling the Mystery

"Mrs. Danvers could you tell us something now?" Colonel Julyan asked.

"Mrs. de Winter despised doctors and never needed one except once when she had sprained her wrist," Mrs. Danvers replied.

"I tell you the fellow is a face-cream mixer, or something of the like," Favell said. "How does it matter?"

"No," said Frank, the porter said he was a well-known women's practioner.

"Hmm, there seems to have been something wrong with her and I wonder that she didn't mention anything, even to Mrs. Danvers," Colonel Julyan deliberated.

"Maybe she went to him for a diet sheet," Favell said. "She was too thin."

Mrs. Danvers seemed bemused and dazed that Rebecca had not mentioned anything to her at all.

"The note," Mrs. Danvers said, "she wanted to tell Mr. Jack something and perhaps me too."

Favell removed the note and read again, *"I've something to tell you and I want to see you as soon as possible. Rebecca."*

I then saw Mrs. Danvers look at Maxim and I realized that it was only now that she was beginning to understand what Favell was getting at. She looked at Maxim with hatred; all the while twisting her dress.

Maxim asked Colonel Julyan if he should go and see the doctor tomorrow.

"He is not going alone," Favell said. "Send Inspector Welch with him."

Colonel Julyan said that Inspector Welch needn't be brought into the picture yet and if it would satisfy Favell if he went with Maxim.

"Yes, I suppose that is all right, but for safety sake would you mind if I come along too?" Favell asked.

"I wouldn't mind, but you must be sober."

It occurred to me that Favell and Frank were only now beginning to understand the significance of her visit to the doctor.

Nine o'clock the next morning was decided. Favell came to shake my hand. I put them behind my back.

"Just too bad," he said. It will be thrilling to see the

yellow press go after you with the headlines, 'From Monte Carlo to Manderley. Experiences of a murderer's girl-bride,' splashed across. Better luck next time."

When Maxim and I were alone I said that I would go with him to London tomorrow morning in the car.

Continuing to look out of the window, Maxim said, "Yes, we must go on being together."

When they all had left, Maxim then came into my arms like a child and for a moment it was as though I was holding Jasper.

"We will sit together driving up to London. Colonel Julyan won't mind. We will have tomorrow night also. They won't do anything immediately. I shall try to get hold of Hastings. He is the best and he used to know my father. Hastings or Birkett."

"Yes," I said.

While we were drinking coffee in the library, Beatrice called. She said that they had received the papers and the verdict was a shock to the both of them. "What does Maxim have to say?" she asked. "It is preposterous, why on earth would she commit suicide? Where is Maxim?"

"Maxim is very tired," I said and "we have to go up to London tomorrow."

"What on earth for?"

"Something to do with the verdict which I can't explain."

"The verdict is absurd and you must get it quashed. Old Horridge must have been off his head. And Julyan? And how can Tabb say whether those holes were deliberate or not? I wish I could have been there. Is Maxim very upset?"

"More tired than upset," I said.

"I wish I could come to London tomorrow but with Roger's fever at 103, I can't see how."

"Can't you get rid of her? What is she saying?" Maxim called to me impatient and annoyed, from the library.

I desperately said, "Beatrice, I will try and ring you up from London."

"Should I speak to Dick Godolphin, your MP?"

"It's no use Beatrice, please don't do anything. It will make matters worse," I said exasperated and thanked God she was not with us today. Something buzzed and the phone went off.

When it rang again, I just let it and after it had stopped Maxim and I sat next to each other, in love and silence.

When I woke up at six o'clock the next morning, there was a foggy dew in the air and the fresh smell of autumn. I could hear Manderley wake up, the smells from the kitchen, the scullery-maids, the gardeners, the curtains being drawn. The birds and bushes going about their business

irrespective of our worries and anxieties.

Manderley had its peace and grace and quiet and all the troubles inside could not mar the loveliness that was outside.

I removed my dressing-case from my wardrobe and began to pack my things in case we had to spend the night in London. My bedroom had the appearance of someone who was going away. I took my hat, gloves and suitcase and went down the stairs. When I was halfway down, I had an urge to go back and look into my room and I did. I looked at the gaping wardrobe and empty bed.

Maxim and I ate breakfast in silence. The car was brought out and Frank came to say that Colonel Julyan was at the gates. He saw no point in driving up. "I shall stand by in the office the whole day for your call. After you have seen Baker, you might want me in London," Frank said.

I asked Frank to take Jasper with him to the office. He looked miserable.

"We better be off," Maxim said.

"You will telephone, won't you?" Frank said.

I turned around and saw Frith and Robert on the stairs and tears welled up in my eyes.

"You will be very tired, I would have taken good care of your husband," Colonel Julyan said as he got into the car.

"I wanted to come," I said.

"That fellow, Favell, said he would wait for us at the crossroads. I do hope he has overslept, we needn't wait for him, if he's not there." But we had no such luck.

We drove and the hours and miles passed.

When we came to Barnet, Colonel Julyan stopped every few minutes to ask for directions. Finally, a postman pointed the house out to us and Maxim parked outside, Favell behind us.

The Colonel suggested we go in.

"I'm ready," said Maxim.

Favell came and said, "What were you all waiting for? Cold feet?"

We were shown in by a maid, then a man of medium height and a long face came out.

"Forgive us this intrusion, Doctor Baker," Colonel Julyan said and made quick introductions. "You may have seen Mr. de Winter's name in the papers recently."

"Oh, yes, something about an inquest. My wife was reading it," he said.

Favell jumped in, "The jury said it was suicide which I believe is not possible and we want to know what she came to you for the day she died."

"You better leave this to the Colonel and me. The

doctor has not the faintest idea what you are saying," Maxim said.

He then explained to the doctor that his late wife's cousin was not happy with the verdict and in her diary, "We found the name and telephone number of your old consulting rooms. She had an appointment with you for two o'clock the day she died and she had kept it. Could you please verify this for us?"

"I am sorry but I have no recollection whatsoever of having seen a Mrs. de Winter," the doctor said.

Colonel Julyan removed the page he had torn from the diary and Doctor Baker agreed that it was his telephone number indeed.

Colonel Juyan asked if it was possible that she might have used a false name.

"That is very possible although we don't encourage that in our profession."

"Would you have a record of her visit? I know it is not etiquette to ask but the circumstances are unusual. We feel that what you say may have a bearing on her suicide," the Colonel said.

"Murder," interrupted Favell.

Doctor Baker raised his eyebrows and gave an inquiring look to Maxim, "I had no idea there was a question of that.

I will do anything in my power to help you. If you will excuse me, I will go up and check my files. I have all the records of the past year."

Doctor Baker came back with large book and file case. He looked up the book and said, "I saw a Mrs. Danvers on the twelfth at two o'clock."

"Danny!" Favell said.

Doctor Baker searched his files and said, "Mrs. Danvers, I remember now."

Colonel Julyan asked, "Tall, slim, dark and handsome?"

"Yes," said the doctor.

The doctor looked into his files and said that this was unprofessional of him because patients are treated like they are in confession and nothing revealed. But he understood that the circumstances were unusual.

"If you believe I can supply a motive as to why your wife must have wanted to take her own life, yes, I can. The woman who called herself Mrs. Danvers was seriously ill," Doctor Baker said.

"Now I remember her perfectly well. She came to me a week before the date you mentioned, for the first time. I took some X-rays. When she came to find out the results of the X-ray, she said that she wanted to hear the truth. She stood it all well, didn't flinch, she had suspected it for

some time; paid my fee and left," Doctor Baker said, shutting his book.

He continued, "The pain was slight, but the growth was deep-rooted. An operation would have been of no use and in three or four months' time she would have been on morphia. The thing had gotten a firm hold and there is nothing that anyone could do.

Outwardly she looked perfectly healthy, although thin and pale, but the X-ray showed a certain malformation of the uterus which meant that she could never have had children. But that is beside the point, it had nothing to do with the disease."

I heard Colonel Julyan thank the doctor and request for a copy of the memoranda. We all shook hands and walked out. "I am happy to have been of use," the doctor said, "It didn't occur to me that Mrs. Danvers and Mrs. de Winter were the same."

Chapter 20

Joy or Sorrow

We all went and stood by the car. Favell looked grey and shaken. He asked, "This cancer business, is it contagious?" Colonel Julyan shrugged his shoulders. "I had not the faintest idea. She kept it a secret even from Danny! Not like Rebecca at all. Cancer! Oh, God!"

"Can you manage your car or would you like Colonel Julyan to drive it for you?" Maxim asked Favell.

"Give me a minute and I'll be fine. This has been an unholy shock."

"Oh, you're fine and your motive has been supplied in black and white. You will dine once a week at Manderley and no doubt Max will ask you to be Godfather to his child," Favell said.

"It's been a stroke of luck for you, Max, but the law can get you and so can I, in a different way."

"If you have anything more to say, please do so now,"

Maxim said.

"No, you can go now," he said stepping back and laughing as we drove away. "He can't do anything, Doctor Baker's evidence will see to it, this smile and threat are all a bluff, they are all the same," Colonel Julyan said.

Maxim was quiet as we drove past telegraph poles, semi-detached villas, motor-coaches and Colonel Julyan asked Maxim if he had no idea at all. "No," said Maxim.

"Some women have a morbid dread of it and she was spared the pain of it all. I will quietly let it be known in Kerrith that a certain doctor had supplied us with the motive, such that the gossip might make it easier on you. Stories sometimes spread like wild fire," he said.

"Yes," said Maxim, "yes, I understand."

"You and Crawley must squash any nonsense at Manderley and the estate."

It was half past six and Colonel Julyan wanted to surprise his sister. Maxim said that he would ever be grateful to Colonel Julyan for today.

When we were alone again, I sank with relief, Maxim put his hand on me but was quiet. Nothing could touch us now; we had come through our crisis.

We got off at a restaurant in a narrow street in Soho and ordered a drink and food. We both needed it. Maxim said that we would put up for the night somewhere and drive to Manderley in the morning.

"Do you suppose Julyan might know the truth," Maxim asked.

"Even if he did, he won't say anything ever," I said.

"I believe that Rebecca lied to me on purpose. The last supreme bluff. She wanted me to kill her and that is why she stood laughing when she died," he said. "It was her last practical joke and I am not sure she hasn't won yet?"

"What do you mean? How can she have won?" I asked.

"I don't know," he said, then got up to ring up Frank.

When he came, he said that Frank was glad and relieved and had been waiting for a call. However, there was something odd.

"Frank believes that Mrs. Danvers has cleared out. Frith called to tell him that she had been packing up the whole day and had stripped her room bare. The fellow from the station had come at four to take her boxes. Frank asked Frith to ask her to come to the office but she did not go. Then at about ten past six there was a long-distance call for her which she had answered in her room. At quarter to seven he knocked on her door but it was empty and she had left. She must have gone through the woods because she didn't use the lodge gates."

I said that that was a good thing as we would anyway have had to send her away. I had kept thinking of the expression on her face last night.

"I don't like it," said Maxim.

"What can she do? Favell must have telephoned. Colonel Julyan said if there was any attempt at blackmail, we should tell him."

"I am not thinking of blackmail," he said.

"What else can they do? As Colonel Julyan said we must forget about it, just go down on our knees and thank God, it is all in the past."

I told him he was tired and needed to eat. I was grateful that Mrs. Danvers had gone, for now I could take command of the house. I thought of redoing the house and having guests over, learning of the estate and gardening and of course, having children.

Suddenly, Maxim pushed his food away and ordered for coffee and the bill. He then asked if I would mind sleeping in the back of the car. He wanted to get to Manderley, he had some feeling. He didn't want to put up anywhere.

"If we start now, at quarter to eight, we can be there by half past two," he said.

"But you will be so terribly tired," I said.

"No, I shall be all right. I want to get home. Something

is wrong and I know it. I want to get home."

His face was strange, he was anxious. I wondered what could be wrong now? I settled myself comfortably at the back of the car and slept.

At half past eleven we were half way home and I said I was thirsty. In the next town, the man at the garage said his wife was not asleep and she would make us some tea. There was a nip in the air and I huddled into my coat. I drank my tea gratefully but Maxim was getting restless.

It was ten minutes to twelve and we drove again, I dreamt of Manderley — there were the woods but no Happy Valley, the nettles were ten foot high.

"Maxim, Maxim," I cried.

"It's all right, I am here."

"I had a dream," I said.

"What was it?"

"I don't know," I said.

I was in the morning room and it was not my handwriting but Rebecca's, I looked into the mirror and the face I saw was Rebecca's. The eyes smiled at me. Maxim was brushing her hair and he twisted it into a thick rope and put it round his neck.

"No, no," I screamed, "we must go to Switzerland, Colonel Julyan said so."

Maxim's hand was upon my face, "What is it?"

"I can't sleep."

"But you have been sleeping. It's quarter past two, you have been sleeping for two hours and we're four miles the other side of Lanyon."

I went and sat beside him and it was very cold, my teeth were chattering.

"What is the time?" I asked.

Twenty past two.

"It's funny, it looks like dawn is breaking over there, beyond those hills, but it is too early."

He did not answer and I watched the sky, the light was spreading across it like sunrise.

"You see the northern lights in winter, don't you? Not in summer, isn't it?"

"That's not northern lights," he said. "That's Manderley."

I saw his face. I saw his eyes.

"Maxim, Maxim, what is it?"

We drove, faster and faster, the road to Manderley lay ahead. There was no moon, the sky above us was inky black but the sky on the horizon was not dark, it was shot with crimson like a splash of blood, the ashes blew towards us with salt wind from the sea as we saw our dear Manderley burning.

Questions

Chapter 1

I. Find the meaning of the following words.

1. Nettles
2. Obstinate
3. Disarray
4. Serenity
5. Desolate

II. Find pictures of the following tress/flowers and stick them in your scrap book.

1. Rhododendrons
2. Ivy
3. Hydrangeas
4. Beeches
5. Chestnut Tree

III. Questions based on the story

1. What happened to the narrator in her dream?
2. How would the narrator like to remember the place she speaks of?

Chapter 2

I. Write the antonyms for the following words:

1. Agony
2. Anonymity
3. Stronger
4. Crisp
5. Feared

II. Fill in the blanks with an appropriate word from the text.

1. Happiness must be ____________.
2. The battle has been ____________.
3. This is a ____________ for the hurt and agony of the past.
4. If you suffer you emerge ____________.
5. I was unsophisticated and awkward and therefore, _______.

III. Questions based on the story

1. What do 'they' look forward to?
2. What would happen at half past four in Manderley?

Chapter 3

I. Match the following words to their meanings.

1. Surreptitiously — a. Showy
2. Unpalatable — b. Secretively
3. Disparage — c. Unappetizing
4. Ostentatious — d. Familiar
5. Acquaintance — e. Depreciate

II. Fill in the following blanks from the text.

The hotel __________ was in _______ ______. The __________ of the hotel reserved his special bow for special customers. Mrs. Van Hopper tapped her _______ against her teeth and she believed that I had ________ the conversation that evening.

III. Questions based on the story.

1. "The waiter having guessed my inferior nature…an hour ago." Write your comments on this statement in four to five lines.
2. Describe, in your own words, Mrs. Van Hopper.

Chapter 4

I. State whether true or false.

1. An empty hotel can be as lonely as a full house.
2. I wanted to go to a cobbled square in Monaco to sketch.
3. You have made a mistake in joining hands with Blaize.
4. I went for lunch a half hour later than usual.
5. I dropped water and the waiter was soaked.

II. Answer briefly:

1. How much did the narrator get paid for her job?
2. Where was Mr. de Winter supposed to have gone that day?
3. Why did Mrs. Van Hopper consider Mr. de Winter important?
4. Who was drowned in the bay near Manderley?
5. Mr. de Winter believed that there was one thing common between him and the narrator. What was it?

III. Questions based on the story

1. What did the narrator reminisce about?
2. Describe briefly, the drive atop the hill undertaken by the narrator and Mr. de Winter.

Chapter 5

I. Find the meanings of the following idioms in the chapter.

1. Serving underhand
2. Still waters run deep
3. Wash my hands off
4. A dark horse
5. Run you down
6. Throwing caution to the wind

II. Fill in the blanks in the following sentences from the chapter.

1. I have been playing ____________ with a professional.
2. A companion is a ____________________.
3. Mrs. Van Hopper and I played ____________ that evening.
4. A phantom was taking shape in my mind. The phantom of ________.
5. Shuffling the cards like an __________________ player.

III. Questions based on the story.

1. Explain "memories in a bottle" in four to five lines in the context of the story.
2. "…and the morning was happy again…" What had made the morning unhappy and why?

Chapter 6

I. Find the meanings of the following words and use them to make sentences of your own.

1. Reverie
2. Diffidence
3. Restraint
4. Philanthropy
5. Trousseau

II. Arrange the following sentences in the order that they were said.

1. We were to leave by a later train but she wants to catch the earlier one.
2. I have gotten used to it.
3. I am afraid it has all been my fault.
4. Don't make a joke of it, I will say good-bye and leave now.
5. You see her, she will be very angry.

III. Questions based on the story.

1. Why were the locks being snapped shut? Where were they going and why?
2. Did the narrator go, eventually? If not, explain briefly, why?

Chapter 7

I. Find words in the chapter that are similar in meanings given below.

1. Stern or strict in manner
2. The exquisite mansion
3. A light, evening meal
4. A series of events performed as per a particular order
5. To recollect past events
6. Unpleasant or disagreeable

II. State whether the following sentences are true or false.

1. We arrived in Manderley at the end of summer.
2. I had been married now for seven weeks.
3. The driveway was a neat broad path of gravel flanked by turf.
4. Mr. and Mrs. de Winter would live in the east wing.
5. Mr. and Mrs. de Winter decided to change for dinner that night.

III. Questions based on the story.

1. Describe the character of Mrs. Danvers. What were your impressions about her?
2. Describe the arrival of Mrs. de Winter to Manderley

Chapter 8

I. Match the words to their meanings.

1. Impose
2. Lingered
3. Docile
4. Tact
5. Resentment

a. Submissive or obedient
b. To be bitter
c. To force upon
d. Reluctant to leave
e. To say something with thoughtfulness

II. Answer in one line.

1. Who came for lunch the next afternoon?
2. What was the fare at breakfast?
3. Who would come for the letters and when?
4. Who did Maxim say had to be visited?
5. What was Beatrice's comment on Maxim's temper?

III. Questions based on the story.

1. Describe the character of Beatrice.
2. What was Beatrice's reaction to seeing the narrator? What were some of the things they spoke of that afternoon?

Chapter 9

I. From the meanings given below, find the appropriate words from the chapter.

1. Fragrant flowers
2. Completely puzzled
3. A small sheltered bay
4. A low area between hills or mountains
2. The speed at which one walks or runs
6. Extremely tired

II. This chapter brings out the beauty of all the five senses – find phrases and sentences that define each of the senses – for e.g.," …rain will bring out the scent of the azaleas…." The sense of smell.

1. smell
2. touch
3. sight
4. taste
5. sound

III. Questions based on the story.

1. What did the narrator find on the other side of the rocks?
2. What is the Happy Valley? Describe it briefly.

Chapter 10

I. Find the meaning of the following words and use them to make sentences of your own.

1. Overwhelming
2. Harbor
3. Buoy
4. Modesty
5. Gauche
6. Cathartic

II. Underline the correct phrase in the following sentences.

1. I asked the chauffer to stop and got off the car to walk with Frank/Maxim.
2. She was found after two/three months near Edgecoombe.
3. Mrs. Danvers had an unpleasantness with Frith/Robert.
4. There were four/five volumes of A History of Painting.
5. I prefer to call on the Bishop's wife/Clarice's mother.

III. Questions based on the story.

1. What made the narrator believe that she was 'so different from Rebecca,' and why?
2. Why did the narrator hide the China Cupid and what happened as a result of it?

Chapter 11

I. Find the meanings of the following words.

1. Jetty
2. Buoy
3. Harbor
4. Cove
5. Shingle

II. Underline the mistake in the following sentences and rewrite the correct answer.

1. "Hello, you little tyke," the man said to me.

2. “Come on, it’s a faster car than what poor old Max has,” he said to Mr. Danvers.
3. “it wouldn’t do good for the mistress of Manderley to be driving with someone,” I said.
4. “I could bring your tea Madam if you like, but it isn’t half past four yet,” Clarice said.
5. “Had I been there, I would not have allowed it,” I said.

III. Questions based on the story.

1. Describe briefly what the narrator found in Rebecca’s room.
2. What was the name of the visitor and why had he come?

Chapter 12

I. Match the following words to their meanings.

1. Propped	a. On time
2. Eton	b. Flew out from a narrow opening
3. Punctual	c. A parade, scene or play
4. Squirted	d. A public school for boys
5. Pageant	e. Supported

II. Answer the following questions briefly.

1. What was served with tea at Gran’s house?
2. What was the name of Gran’s parlor maid?
3. After tea, whom did Gran want?
4. Who did Beatrice say would be angry with her?
5. What did the narrator not want Maxim to know?

III. Questions based on the story.

1. Reflect, in your own words, “I felt sorry for the old lady….,” & “I wondered at the feelings of old people,” why she felt sorry for the old lady and your views on old people.
2. Why was Maxim angry and with whom?

Chapter 13

I. Match the following words to their meanings.

1. Austere	a. To bombard
2. Minstrel’s gallery	b. To be helpful or kind knowing your superiority
3. Perquisite	c. Benefit or advantage
4. Patronized	d. Stern, unfeeling
5. Barrage	e. A balcony inside a castle or mansion

II. Answer in brief.

1. Who insisted on the fancy-dress ball?
2. What did she want the narrator to dress as?
3. What did Mr. de Winter want her to dress as?
4. Who suggested that the narrator have a look at the minstrel's gallery?
5. Who was going to be dressed as an Arabian Sheikh?

III. Questions Based on the Story.

1. Describe briefly how Manderley was getting ready for the ball?
2. Why was the narrator excited about her costume and what did she want to do?

Chapter 14

I. Arrange the following sentences in the sequence that they took place in the story.

1. I looked down from my window at the rose garden and saw the men inspecting the lights as they were coming on.
2. I knew this was a terrible mistake and you could not have known, how would you?
3. She kept saying that it is she who should be thanked for the ball and not the de Winters.
4. Please sit a while, you look very ill.
5. The board creaked when I had not even moved.

II. Questions based on the story.

1. Was Mr. Maxim de Winter justified in being angry with Mrs. de Winter? Give reasons for your answer.
2. What were some of the highlights of that evening?

Chapter 15

I. Find the meanings of the following words and use them to make sentences of your own.

1. Convention
2. Derided
3. Crew
4. Coast guard
5. Deceitful

II. Mixed Bag.

1. "I could feel her presence everywhere and she could feel mine." The presence here is Mrs. Danvers or Rebecca?
2. Suddenly, the silence was broken by an ____________.

   (Fill in the blanks)
3. Explain, 'to hold in high regard.'

4. What are winkles?
5. Captain ________ was the _______ master from ___________.
   (Fill in the blanks)

III. Questions based on the story

1. What revelation is the narrator shocked to hear? Explain the circumstances in brief.
2. What does Mrs. Danvers want the narrator to do? Explain the episode briefly.

Chapter 16

I. Make sentences with the following words/idioms/phrases/proverbs.

1. Time and tide wait for no man
2. Turn a new life
3. Bewildered
4. Mocking
5. Laugh behind someone's back

II. Answer briefly.

1. Who were the people present when the boat was raised?
2. Who came for lunch that afternoon?
3. What did the narrator want Mrs. Danvers to do?
4. Who is an 'heir?'
5. They got calls from the newspapers. What term is used to define the press? The ______ ________.

III. Questions based on the story.

1. Explain briefly why Mr. de Winter felt compelled to do what he did. According to you, was it justified?
2. How had the narrator changed in the course of twenty-four hours? Support your answer with examples.

Chapter 17

I. Give one antonym and one synonym for the following words.

Words	Synonym	Antonym
Distressed		
Expectant		
Identify		
Sympathy		
Starting		

Arrange the following sentences in the order that they happen:

1. I was getting very restless and walked to the passage.
2. There was a great column and a blurred picture of Maxim taken some fifteen years ago.
3. "It's over," he said. "Suicide."
4. "Will someone take my wife outside?"
5. I asked Robert if the men were back and he said no.

III. Questions based on the story.

1. Describe briefly, the Inquest?
2. To distract herself who did the narrator begin to think of and in what way?

Chapter 18

I. Homophones are words that sound the same but have different spellings and meanings. Given below are a list of words from the chapter. Find the homophone and use it in a sentence of your own. One has been done for you.

Here	hear	The dog did not hear my footsteps.
See		
Right		
Weather		
Wait		
Night		

II. Who said the following lines?

1. Get me a witness.
2. I wanted to tackle de Winter personally.
3. She's gone.
4. He can't twist things around and make things difficult for you.
5. Try museum.

III. Questions based on the story.

1. Who summoned Captain Julyan and why?
2. What is blackmail? Who was blackmailing whom and why?

Chapter 19

I. Explain the following terms.

1. To buy time
2. Yellow Press

3. Preposterous
4. Exasperated
5. Cold feet

II. Answer briefly.

1. Who was going to London?
2. Why were they going?
3. At what time did they reach London?
4. What is etiquette and what was considered to be bad etiquette?
5. Who did the doctor say he had seen on the said day at two o' clock?

III. Questions based on the story.

1. What did their visit to London reveal?
2. What are your views on the revelations that were made?

Chapter 20

I. Explain the following terms.

1. Out of sight is out of mind
2. Count on you
3. Northern Lights
4. Motive
5. Spread like wild fire

II. Fill in the blanks.

1. We dropped Colonel Julyan at __________.
2. Frank believes that ______________ has cleared out.
3. It looks like ________ is breaking over there.
4. I drank my tea ___________ but Maxim was getting _________.
5. We're ________ miles, the other side of ___________.

III. Questions based on the story.

1. What is the joy and what the sorrow in this chapter?
2. Do you believe that Rebecca did eventually win, in this novel?

Titles in this Series:

1. The Jungle Book
2. The Wizard of Oz
3. Gulliver's Travels
4. Black Beauty
5. A Christmas Carol
6. Dracula
7. Robinson Crusoe
8. Little Women
9. The Time Machine
10. Heidi
11. Don Quixote
12. Kim
13. Rebecca
14. The Invisible Man
15. Three Men in a Boat
16. Treasure Island
17. Pride & Prejudice
18. A Tale of Two Cities
19. Oliver Twist
20. Kidnapped
21. Wuthering Heights
22. King Solomon's Mines
23. Moby Dick
24. Jane Eyre
25. The Wind in the Willows
26. The Three Musketeers
27. The Call of the Wild
28. Frankenstein
29. Pollyanna
30. Peter Pan
31. The Secret Garden
32. The Picture of Dorian Gray
33. The Hound of the Baskervilles
34. Alice's Adventures in Wonderland
35. The Adventures of Tom Sawyer
36. The Adventures of Sherlock Holmes
37. The Memoirs of Sherlock Holmes
38. The Adventures of Huckleberry Finn
39. The Hunchback of Notre Dame
40. Great Expectations
41. Around the World in 80 Days
42. The Strange Case of Dr. Jekyll and Mr. Hyde
43. The Adventures of Robinhood
44. A Journey to the Center of the Earth
45. Twenty Thousand Leagues Under the Sea
46. The Phantom of the Opera
47. The Prince and the Pauper
48. The Count of Monte Christo
49. The Swiss Family Robinson
50. Tales of Mystery and Horror